NO ESCAPE

The warrior who had spotted Davy charged, waving a tomahawk. Flavius knew his friend could never reload in time. He fired on the fly. Maybe he wasn't a match for Crockett, who had won more shooting matches than any backwoodsman in all of Tennessee, but he was no slouch, either. His bullet crumpled the onrushing hostile in mid-stride.

Then Davy was among the Indians, swinging his heavy rifle as if it were a club, knocking painted figures aside right and left. The last man reared to stop him. There was a fleeting image of an angular head shaven bald except for a ridge of hair down the center, of a porcupine hair roach decorated with feathers. A heartbeat later the sorrel's shoulder caught the warrior in the chest and he went tumbling.

Reining in sharply, Davy sped toward the tree line and welcome cover—just as more warriors poured from the forest.

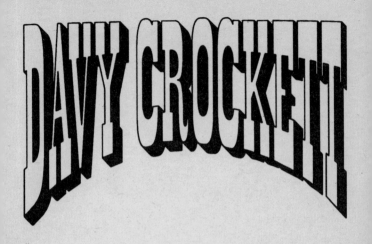

HOMECOMING

David Thompson

LEISURE BOOKS ⬛ NEW YORK CITY

To Judy, Joshua, and Shane.

A LEISURE BOOK®

November 1996

Published by

Dorchester Publishing Co., Inc.
276 Fifth Avenue
New York, NY 10001

Printed in the United States of America.

HOMECOMING

Chapter One

Davy Crockett reined up the instant he heard a twig snap, his right hand tightening on the long rifle he had named Liz in honor of his second wife. Blue eyes narrowing, he studied the dense growth on both sides of the game trail. His every instinct told him that something, or someone, was out there.

Just at that moment loud whistling broke out behind the muscular frontiersman. It was the tune to a bawdy ballad popular in taverns from Tennessee to Maine. Crockett glared at his traveling companion and whispered, "Consarn it! Hush, you blamed varmint!"

Flavius Harris glanced up, startled. One year younger than Crockett, he was as plump as an overripe pear. He had been idly daydreaming about how nice it would be to have heaping helpings of rabbit or squirrel stew for their supper, and did not understand why his friend was so upset with him. "What has you in such a huff?" he called out loudly.

Davy Crockett sighed. There were times when he was pretty near convinced that his friend had been off playing in a turnip patch when the Almighty passed out brains. Putting a finger to his lips, he pointed at the dense woods.

Flavius quieted. If there was one thing he had learned about David Crockett, it was that the brawny Irishman had few peers when it came to wilderness savvy. Firmly clutching his Kentucky rifle, he licked his thick lips and prayed that they weren't about to get into another scrape.

To the east Davy detected movement, the furtive flitting of a two-legged figure closing in on them. Applying his heels to his sorrel, he broke into a gallop and hollered, "Indians!"

That was all Flavius had to hear. His dun exploded when he slammed his heels into its flanks. Lashing his reins like a madman, Flavius stayed close enough to Davy's sorrel to count the hairs in its tail. Come what may, he wasn't about to get separated from Davy. It would take him forever to find his way back to Tennessee by his lonesome.

Wild whoops rent the air. Painted forms sprouted on the right and left. Davy automatically ducked low just as an arrow cleaved the space his torso had occupied. The narrow trail turned sharply to the west. As the sorrel pounded past the bend, a swarthy warrior loomed out of the high brush, a war club raised to strike.

Davy had only a fleeting glimpse of his attacker. Before the club could descend, he lashed downward with his rifle. The stock crunched against the man's face. Another second and Davy was in the clear. He saw the warrior totter backward, the war club all but forgotten.

Flavius kicked at the bloody Indian as he went by, but the man was too far off. A glittering shaft whizzed past his cheek, reminding him of the broad target his backside made. He reapplied his reins to the dun.

In another forty feet Davy swept around a second bend. The war whoops were already tapering off. He held to a gallop, though, until they had traveled half a mile. In a verdant meadow rife with high grass he finally drew rein, then turned the sorrel so he could survey the country they had just covered. "I reckon we gave them the slip," he declared.

Mightily pleased to hear it, Flavius wiped a buckskin-clad sleeve across his perspiring brow. He noticed that his friend's cheeks were as red as beets.

Anyone who did not know Crockett as well as Flavius would assume that Davy was flushed from excitement. But the truth was that Crockett's cheeks were always extremely ruddy, so much so that many people could not help commenting on the fact when they met him for the first time. Davy had once mentioned being that way since birth and having no idea what it meant. Flavius suspected it had something to do with why his friend had three times the stamina of most men and had never been sick a day in his life, except for a few recent bouts of weakness and fever that never lasted very long.

Suddenly Flavius became aware that Davy was speaking.

"—light out for that hill yonder and scout the area

for more hostiles. What do you say?"

"Where you go, I go," Flavius answered.

Davy rode on. The presence of the war party did not particularly disturb him. None of the Indians in that part of the country possessed horses, and there wasn't a man born, red or white, who could catch his sorrel once he gave the animal its head.

Flavius reached into a leather bag slanted across his chest, between his powder horn and bullet pouch, and helped himself to a strip of jerky. "What tribe were they?"

"I don't rightly know," Davy admitted. Since leaving his cabin weeks ago, they had run into a heap of Indians. Most had proven friendly. The few tribes not partial to whites had been so obvious about it that he had lit a shuck for somewhere else before they could take a tomahawk to his noggin.

A more important question occurred to Flavius. "I've been meaning to ask. How much longer are we going to be on this gallivant of yours anyhow? I told Matilda that we'd be back before the next full moon, but it appears to me that I'll miss the mark by a month or better."

"Afraid she'll wallop the tar out of you when we do show up?"

Flavius snorted. "Me? Afeared of a contrary female? Heck, no. I wear the britches in our home, not her. And I'll thrash any coon who claims different!"

Davy made no comment, but a grin curled his mouth. It was common knowledge throughout middle and west Tennessee that Flavius Harris had married a regular ring-tailed snorter. Which was putting it delicately. Many a time, Flavius's neighbors had seen him hightailing it across his fields with Matilda in furious pursuit, her rolling pin hoisted to brain him if he so much as slowed to catch his breath.

"Besides," Flavius went on slyly, "if she gets her dander up, all I have to do is fetch her a few store-boughten gewgaws, and she'll calm down faster than a wildcat dunked in water."

The hill lay a quarter of a mile to the northwest. At its base grew tall pines. Boulders dotted the summit. Davy ground-hitched his sorrel among the trees and padded up the slope, straining his ears to catch the slightest sound. Other than the huffing and puffing of his friend, the wilderness lay quiet under the midday sun.

It was *too* quiet, Davy reflected. There should be squirrels chattering, birds chirping, insects buzzing. Yet the forest beyond the hill was as still as a graveyard at midnight.

Hunkering in the shadow of a boulder, Davy scanned the terrain below. Lush woodland was bisected by numerous creeks, creating a hunter's paradise. Glancing over his shoulder, he could see, far to the south, the gleaming surface of Lake Superior.

Davy's first sight of the Great Lakes, days ago, had been a grand experience. It had reminded him of the very first time he'd set eyes on the ocean, back when he was fourteen or so. He'd been in Baltimore, adrift from his family and making ends meet as best he could. One day he'd ambled down to the wharf, where the huge ships with their fluttering sails had stirred him so deeply that he'd been all fired up to take to a life at sea. He'd even gone so far as to agree to hire on as the cabin boy on a vessel bound for London. But things hadn't worked out. If they had, he'd probably be taking his ease on a South Seas island instead of traipsing all over creation.

Flavius Harris could not understand why his friend was dawdling. His mouth crammed with jerked venison, he remarked, "It looks peaceable enough down there. Let's go find us a good spot and make an early camp." He paused to pry a tiny piece of jerky from between his front teeth. "I sure would admire to treat ourselves to a big pot of rabbit stew tonight. Or maybe you could rustle up a buck! I'd fix a feast fit for royalty. What do you say?"

It never ceased to amaze Davy. All his companion ever thought of was food, food, and more food. Flavius wasn't a glutton, exactly, but there was no denying that the jovial woodsman was more fond of eating than he was of anything else.

Not that Davy would ever carp about it. He had too many faults of his own to pick on anyone else. Prime among them was his incurable wanderlust. Here he was, a married man with young children to look after, and he was forever going off to hunt or explore or make war or some such nonsense.

Time and again his conscience would prick him. He knew his rightful place was home with Elizabeth and their brood, yet he could no more control his cravings to roam than he could stop breathing.

One day, Davy mused, his hankering to always see what lay over the next hill was liable to be the death of him.

Just then a sound wafted on the breeze. It was not one Crockett expected to hear. Stiffening, convinced his ears were playing tricks on him, he cocked his head. There it was again!

Flavius stopped chewing. "Am I addlepated, or do I hear what I think I hear?"

"You do, hoss," Davy confirmed.

Again the wind from the northwest bore the merry tinkle of laughter. Pleasant, silken, *female* laughter.

"We must be near a village!" Flavius declared, conjuring a mental picture of a horde of bloodthirsty savages swooping down on them. "We'd best light a rag while we still have our scalps!"

"Calm down," Davy said. He doubted very much that they had stumbled on an Indian encampment. For one thing, no smoke tendrils spiraled skyward. For another, no dogs were yapping, no children frolicking about.

"It must be the village those warriors are from," Flavius said, his anxiety mounting. "We linger, and they're liable to stake us out and whittle on us to test our courage."

Davy motioned for silence. A pair of women had appeared near the hill. One had gray hair and carried a basket. The other was as lovely an Indian maiden as ever was born, with long raven tresses and a buckskin dress that clung to her full form as if she was ripe to burst.

"Land sakes!" Flavius said. "Ain't that filly a beauty!"

The women appeared to be gathering herbs. The oldest did most of the searching and digging, while the youngest chatted happily. A few snatches of conversation carried up to Davy, but their tongue was unfamiliar.

Unexpectedly, the older woman pointed at the hill and headed toward it.

Davy flattened, then crawled backward until he could rise with no risk of being spotted. "You get your wish," he whispered to Flavius. "We'll make ourselves scarce."

Making no more noise than the wind itself, they crept to their horses and mounted. Davy threaded through the trees, bearing westward, his intention being to skirt the hill and enter the forest at a point where they would be screened from the women.

Flavius, leaning back to reach into his saddlebags for a twist of chewing tobacco, happened to gaze to the south. His pulse quickened when he discovered a knot of warriors jogging in their direction. It had to be the same war party they had tangled with earlier. "Crockett!" he whispered.

Davy took one look, and was about to goad his sorrel into a trot when a piercing scream from the other side of the hill stopped him cold. It was followed by outraged voices and gruff laughter. Without hesitation, he reined to the right.

"What the—!" Flavius exclaimed, then followed suit. Long ago he had learned that when folks were in trouble, his partner was always ready to lend a hand. Several times Davy's charitable streak had nearly gotten them killed, but that didn't stop Davy from wading right in again when the need arose. It was enough to give a sensible man fits.

The sorrel pounded past a spruce. Davy saw six or seven warriors grappling with the two females halfway up the slope. The older woman had dropped her basket and was trying to claw the eyes from a hefty specimen armed with a long knife. At the same time, three other men were attempting to pin the young maiden, who resisted fiercely. The trio were laughing heartily, making so much noise that Davy covered thirty more feet before one of the warriors heard the drum of the sorrel's hooves and turned.

The old woman had angered the man with the knife, who hefted it high for a fatal stab. Instantly Davy's long rifle leaped to his shoulder. He took a hasty bead and curled back the hammer, stroking the trigger as the knife arced downward. The ball took the man high in the shoulder, spinning him completely around. In a twinkling, the old woman scrambled upright and dashed to the aid of the maiden.

The warrior who had spotted Davy charged, waving a tomahawk. Flavius knew his friend could never reload in time. He fired on the fly. Maybe he wasn't a match for Crockett, who had won more shooting matches than any backwoodsman in all of Tennessee, but he was no slouch either. His bullet crumpled the onrushing hostile in midstride.

Then Davy was among the Indians, swinging Liz as if the heavy rifle were a club, knocking painted figures aside right and left. The last man reared to stop him. There was a fleeting image of an angular head shaven bald except for a ridge of hair down the center, of a porcupine hair roach decorated with feathers. A heartbeat later the sorrel's shoulder caught the warrior in the chest and he went tumbling.

For a few moments the women were in the clear. Davy leaned over as the young one stood, his left arm hooking her slender waist. He flung her over the front

15

of his saddle none too gently, while bawling, "Flavius! Grab the other one!"

Reining sharply, Davy sped toward the tree line and welcome cover—just as more warriors poured from the forest.

Chapter Two

"He who hesitates is lost" was a saying as old as the hills of Tennessee. It was one Davy Crockett had taken to heart. Many was the time he had pulled his bacon out of the fire by acting on the spur of the moment when his life was in danger. Harsh experience had taught him that in the wilderness a man's reflexes often meant the difference between life and death.

So as the ragged line of howling warriors burst from the woods, Davy did not waste precious moments debating what he should do. He barreled right into them, the sorrel a living battering ram that scattered the warriors like chaff before a strong wind.

Cries of outrage and a few flying shafts followed Davy into the woods. He glanced at the beautiful young maiden to see if she was all right. Mouth agape, she gawked at him in utter amazement. "I'm a friend," he said to reassure her, but she went on gaping. He

17

shifted her higher to relieve the strain on his shoulder, then thought of his friend. Had Flavius gotten away too?

At that moment the object of Davy's concern had his hands full. Literally. As Crockett had directed, Flavius had leaned way down to scoop the older woman into his arm. But where the young maiden had gone rigid with astonishment and not offered a lick of resistance, the older woman proved to be a regular wildcat.

Hissing and screeching, the woman scratched at Flavius. Her nails raked his full cheeks, his forehead. One narrowly missed an eye.

"Simmer down, you ornery cuss!" Flavius hollered. Temporarily unable to see where he was going, he let the dun have its head, counting on it to stay close to Davy's mount, while he struggled mightily to keep from losing his grip on the female. Almost at his elbow a warrior whooped and something thudded against Flavius's thigh. Pain lanced through him.

Flavius jerked the reins to the left, then to the right. He had no idea where he was going. His intention was to make himself harder to hit.

Then the dun took a wild bound to clear an obstacle in front of them. The jolt jarred the old woman across the saddle, allowing Flavius to see that they had streaked into the woods. He also discovered, to his horror, that Davy was nowhere in sight.

"No!" Flavius squawked, anxiously scanning the vegetation. It scared him pea-green to think that the fate he most feared had come to pass. "Davy!" he bawled, his anxiety mounting when he received no reply.

The shout sparked the old woman to life. Barking like a rabid mongrel, she struck at his chest and shoulders, seeking to break free. Flavius had half a mind to grant her wish and dump her on her backside. But Davy would be all het up if he did, so he clung on while frantically scouring the verdant landscape.

Flavius almost called his friend's name again, but thought better of the notion. There might be more of those bloodthirsty warriors about and the last thing he wanted was to tangle with another pack of red demons.

His thigh throbbed. No blood showed, nor was his legging torn. Apparently a war club had struck him, not a lance or arrow. Thank God.

Grimacing, Flavius cut to the south, seeking sign. In a dozen yards he swung northward again. His heart hammered in his chest, his temples pounding so loudly that he could barely hear the furious caterwauling of the old woman. He had to find Davy. He just *had* to.

Unknown to the portly backwoodsman, Davy Crockett was thinking the same thing about him. Davy had slowed and twisted in the saddle.

So far there was no sign of pursuit. In itself that was a minor puzzlement since the warriors had not impressed him as the sort to give up easily.

Davy took a gamble. In order to allow his friend to catch up, he halted in a small clearing. The breeze had died, and the forest was as quiet as a church in the middle of a parson's sermon. Convinced he could hear trouble coming long before it reached them, he carefully lowered the maiden and slid off the sorrel.

Davy had another reason for wanting to stop. It didn't do for a frontiersman to go around with an empty gun. His rifle had to be reloaded, and quickly, in case more hostiles showed up. Fingers flying, he opened his powder horn and poured the proper amount of black powder into the muzzle. Next he used the ramrod to feed a patch and ball down the barrel.

The maiden watched his every movement. She stood calmly, her arms at her sides, no fear evident. Up close, it was apparent her dress was of the very finest buckskin. The front had been adorned with masterful beadwork, as well as the hem.

Her composure impressed Davy. He smiled once more, but received no response. "I mean you no harm," he said. On getting no reply, he asked while closing the flap on his bullet pouch, "Do you savvy the white man's tongue, miss?"

Davy did not really expect her to answer. Other than a few missionaries and trappers, the Indians in that part of the country had not had much contact with whites. So he was all the more surprised when she cleared her throat and spoke in thickly accented English.

"Yes. Little bit."

Elated, Davy impulsively grasped her warm hand. "Land sakes alive! Wherever did you learn it?"

The maiden looked down, her brow furrowed, but made no attempt to pull loose. "Man who wear long dress teach," she said.

"Long dress?" Davy repeated, mystified until she made the sign of a cross in the air. "Oh. You mean a

Bible-thumper. Does he live hereabouts?"

"Him dead."

A troubling thought occurred to Davy. Some missionaries had more zeal than common sense. They tried to force their doctrine down the throats of the tribes they were sent to convert, with disastrous results.

With his own eyes, Davy had once witnessed a minister railing at the Creeks for being a nation of "worthless heathens," "vermin doomed to suffer the fires of Hell" unless they repented their sins and "bowed before the true God of the white man." That minister never had understood why none of the Creeks came forward afterward to be baptized.

"Did your people make wolf meat of the man in the long dress?" Davy inquired.

"Wolf meat? Oh, no. Winnebagos kill," the woman revealed.

Davy was relieved. Sometimes a single white man could sour relations with a tribe so badly that any whites who came along later were apt to find themselves turned into pincushions for no other crime than the color of their skin.

A case in point was Meriwether Lewis, the famous explorer. On the way back from the epic Lewis and Clark expedition to the Pacific Ocean, Lewis and his men had slain a couple of Blackfeet. Ever since, the Blackfeet had had it in for any whites caught in their territory.

"Who you be?" the maiden asked.

He told her his name, adding, "My partner and I are traipsing around the country to see what there is to see. It's lucky for you that we came along when we did. Those fellers with the Mohawk hair weren't acting none too friendly." She gave him a curious stare, and it hit him that she probably had never heard of the Mohawks. Rather than explain, he asked, "What might your name be?"

"Wawaneechotinka."

Davy blinked. Some Indian names were a mouthful, but hers was big enough to choke a hog. "What tribe are you from?"

"Ojibwas."

The name rang a bell. Most whites called them the Chippewas. They claimed a wide region north of the Great Lakes as their own, and had been able to hold it against all aggressors. "Is your village nearby?" Davy asked.

Wawaneechotinka made note of the position of the sun, then pointed to the northwest. "That way."

A decision had to be made. It was best that she be returned to her people before they came looking for her, but Davy was loath to ride off without Flavius. He rose onto the tips of his toes to study their back trail. "Who were those warriors trying to take you captive?"

"Fox men."

Davy seemed to recollect that a tribe by that name and another called the Sauks were bitter enemies of the Chippewas and their allies, the Dakotas and the Iowas. They were also not very fond of whites. "Your people have to be warned that there is a war party in the area," he commented.

Wawaneechotinka also surveyed the woodland to the south. "Kiyo Kaga never come this far before."

"Who?"

"Chief of Fox tribe. Him hate all Ojibwas. Want to wipe us out."

It was the same story Davy had heard many times before. Just like his own kind, Indian tribes were always at each other's throats. Hurons against Iroquois. Mohawks against Micmacs. The Seminoles against tribes south of them in the Territory of Florida.

Davy never had been fond of warfare. True, he'd enlisted to fight in the Creek War, but he'd soon had his fill of the hardship and bloodshed. To his way of thinking, war was a terrible waste. It used men up like cannon fodder, often leaving the victors little better off than the losers.

Still nothing stirred in the surrounding woods. Davy began to pace, debating whether to go hunt Flavius up or to wait a while longer. "Where can that blamed pumpkin be?" he wondered, praying that his pard had not gotten himself rubbed out.

At that very moment, Flavius Harris was asking himself, "Where in tarnation am I?" as the dun crossed a narrow field. He had yet to come on his friend's tracks, and he fretted that he was straying wider of the mark with every step his horse took.

The old woman had quieted down for a bit, but now she surged into violent motion, swatting at his belly even as she tried to push off and drop to the ground. Flavius held her in place with an effort. For such a scrawny thing, she was incredibly spry. He doubted that he could hold her down if she were a few years younger.

Entering a tract of oaks, Flavius drew rein to listen. Other than the buzz of a bee busy in a nearby patch of wildflowers, the forest appeared empty of living creatures. The gunshots and war whoops had frightened them off or driven them into hiding.

The old woman churned her legs and arms, redoubling her efforts to escape. Her movements caused Flavius's hand to slip off her back. As it did, she rolled onto her side. His hand wound up on her breast, and it was hard to say which of them was more shocked. She turned bright red, then sputtered like a boiler about to rupture at the seams.

Appalled, Flavius jerked his hand away as if he had just set it on a water moccasin. "Sorry, ma'am!" he exclaimed, feeling his ears become as hot as burning coals.

If there was one lesson his ma had taught him, it was to always respect womanhood. "Don't you be like other men," she had frequently scolded when he first started to court the local fillies. "Don't be pawing any girl without her say-so. And whatever you do, don't force yourself on a woman. No man worthy of the name would ever stoop so low."

His mother did not know it at the time, but she had nothing to fear in that regard. Flavius had always been shy around the opposite sex. So much so that he'd become all tongue-tied whenever he took a girl to a social or went on a picnic. Some of them had taken to laughing at him behind his back, saying he was as shy as a ringnecked pheasant. Which had hurt him deeply.

Meeting Matilda had been a revelation. She talked enough for the two of them combined, and she never seemed to mind that he seldom got a word in edgewise.

As for touching each other, Matilda had laid down

the law their second time out. "I might as well make it plain so I won't have to bust your head wide open some day," she'd informed him. "I'll let you know when I'm feeling frisky. Try to kiss me when I'm not and I'll knock your teeth down your throat. Is that clear?"

Flavius had been handling the reins of a rented buggy at the time. Her bluntness had nearly startled him into dropping them, but somehow he had kept a stone face and answered with what was to become his pet expression over the years. "Whatever you say, my dear."

Before they wed, Flavius could count the number of times she let him embrace her on one hand. He'd figured that it would be pretty much the same after their marriage, but she had turned into an inferno of passion, demanding that he "cuddle" her two or three times a week, much to his delight.

He knew that other men poked fun at him for being married to such a shrew. Little did they realize that there was much more to Matilda than met the eye.

Flavius's fleeting remembrance was cut short by the old Indian woman, who shoved him so hard that he nearly pitched backward. She slid off before he could recover and darted into the brush with the speed of a spooked doe.

"Good riddance," Flavius grumbled. He was not going to try to fetch her back. Why should he, when for all he had done on her behalf she wanted to rip his eyes out?

"I've got to catch up with Davy," he said to himself.

Since the old woman had gone off to the northwest, Flavius headed to the northeast. He trotted along for

25

the better part of half an hour without coming on a trace of his companion. The woodland became lowland terrain dotted with streams and shallow lakes. Repeatedly he had to ford waterways, and each instance made him as nervous as a cat in a room full of rocking chairs.

Water had never been Flavius's favorite element. As a child of six he had nearly drowned in a flood-swollen creek. It had so rattled him that forever after he fought shy of water, refusing to even bathe unless forced.

He'd never learned to swim. When the other boys had gone to the river to frolic on a hot summer's day, he'd spied on them, envying their happiness, wishing he could marshal the courage to join in. He never had.

As a result, Flavius had an abiding fear of drowning. Whenever he crossed a stream, he worried that his horse would step into a sinkhole. His buckskins became clammy from cold sweat.

Presently a wide lake loomed before him. Flavius considered skirting it, but the shore was dotted by treacherous bogs that might suck him under. Since the lake did not seem all that deep, he reluctantly nudged the dun in.

All went well for a while. The clear water enabled Flavius to pick his way. Any murky spots or areas where the depth seemed to increase were diligently avoided. Once he spotted a sinuous shape to his right. He brought up his rifle, then recalled that he had failed to reload. His hand swooped to a pistol. Fortunately, the snake submerged, heading away from him.

"Lord, I hate this," Flavius muttered. He'd rather wrestle a riled bear. Once he reached dry land, he'd stick to the shore, bogs or no bogs.

Homecoming

The dun reached the middle and kept on going. Ears pricked, it behaved as nervously as Flavius. Suddenly a short silver form flitted past. A fish, Flavius reckoned. The dun shied, but he kneed it forward, speaking quietly to soothe it. When another fish swam on by, the horse stopped dead and nickered.

"It's all right," Flavius said, patting the animal's neck. "We've nothing to worry about."

As if to prove him wrong, an entire school picked that moment to flash across their path. The dun whinnied louder and reared, its front legs windmilling.

"Damn!" Flavius bellowed, resisting gravity for all he was worth. Gravity won. The next moment water closed over him. His feet found purchase and he attempted to straighten. Too late, he saw the dun's rear hoof angling at his head.

A mile to the south, Davy Crockett stopped pacing and climbed onto the sorrel. "I reckon I have to go find my friend. He should be with that other woman—"

"My mother," Wawaneechotinka said.

Davy pursed his lips. Flavius's absence weighed heavily on his conscience. Should anything have happened, it would be his fault for dragging Flavius off to parts unknown. "You're welcome to come if you'd like," he said, extending his arm.

Wawaneechotinka did not hesitate. Swinging lithely up behind him, she wrapped her arms around his waist. Her bosom pressed against his back. "Kiyo Kaga catch them, he kill them," she declared.

Davy did not point it out, but Kiyo Kaga would do the same to them if they were caught. Any man with half a brain would get out of there while he could. But

Davy could no more abandon Flavius than he could stop breathing. It just wasn't in his nature.

There was more involved than friendship. Simply put, it was the right thing to do. And come what may, Davy had long ago decided to live his life by the principle of always doing what he saw as right no matter how it might effect him.

His folks had to take some of the credit. Particularly his pa, who had hammered into his skull the same saying a million times: "Always be sure you're right, then go ahead and do what has to be done."

It was the motto Davy lived by. Some of his neighbors in Tennessee branded him as crazy as a betsy bug. Others were of the opinion that he was too high and mighty in his ways. Both failed to see that having a code to live by was what distinguished humankind from the beasts.

A hungry panther never changed its mind about killing prey because it realized that killing was wrong. A cottonmouth never refused to strike because inflicting harm on others was an evil act.

Only a human being—specifically a person with character—could tell the difference between right and wrong.

The flutter of wings shattered Davy's reverie. Chiding himself for letting his attention stray, he slowed to a walk to avoid blundering into an ambush. Wawaneechotinka was peering over his shoulder, her breath lightly caressing his cheek. The sensation was awfully distracting, but he did not complain.

Without warning, her lips brushed his ear. "Why you help me, Red Cheeks?" she whispered.

It was hardly the best time or place to go into a long-winded explanation, so Davy replied, "You needed it. Anyone in your tribe would have done the same."

"But you not Ojibwa. You are stranger."

Davy's ear tingled with every syllable. He squirmed, and had to force himself to concentrate on the lay of the land. "Where I come from, a man is supposed to help anyone in need. Whether he knows them or not." He paused. "Isn't it the same with your people?"

"Ojibwas help Ojibwas. Ojibwas help Dakotas. Ojibwas not help anyone else."

"That's the trouble with this old world. Too many strangers and not enough friends."

Wawaneechotinka took a breath as if to say more, but froze when undergrowth to their north crackled with the passage of something large.

Instantly Davy brought the sorrel to a stop and trained his rifle on the spot. He would rather not shoot if he could help it since the shot would bring the rest of the Fox warriors down on their heads like a swarm of mad red ants. Every nerve jangling, he glued his eyes to a patch of quivering weeds.

Into the open poked the head of a young moose. It regarded them with casual interest, shook its ungainly head as if in disapproval, and ambled off, making enough noise to be heard clear back in Tennessee.

That was a moose for you, Davy reflected. So big and powerful that they tramped around like they were the lords of creation. Temperamental cusses too. Thankfully, this one had not decided to attack.

Wawaneechotinka said a few words in her own tongue, then reverted to English. "Manitou send moose. To warn us."

"What's a manitou?" Davy asked.

The maiden encompassed the forest with a sweep of her shapely arm. She indicated the azure sky, the velvet green of a distant hill. She pointed at a red hawk soaring on high, at a flock of sparrows flitting in the trees. "Manitou," she said. "Whites call God. Man in long dress call Father. Ojibwas call Manitou."

Davy never ceased to be amazed by how religious many tribes were. Some were as devoted to their beliefs as the folks back home who occupied the amen pews in church every Sunday, the ones who always prayed and sang the loudest.

He himself had never made any pretensions to be overly godly. Any leanings he had were more the result of the women in his life than his own inclinations. His first wife, Polly, had been uncommonly spiritual, as was his current wife, Elizabeth. He liked to think that they made up for any defect of his that might have a bad influence on their children.

"We must go," Wawaneechotinka whispered. "Come back with many Ojibwas."

Davy clucked to the sorrel. "I'd like to oblige you," he said. But he never had been much of a believer in signs and portents. A moose was just a moose. That one had crossed their path was coincidence, nothing more. "I can't, though. You're welcome to hop off and skedaddle to your village if you want. I won't hold it against you."

Her answer was a long time in coming. "I stay, Red Cheeks. But we both be sorry."

Relying on all the stealth at his command, Davy slowly approached the hill where he had last seen Flavius. There was bound to be sign of a struggle if the Fox band had caught him. Trailing them would pose no problem with their tracks so fresh. All he had to do was hang back until dark, then move in and rescue his friend.

The sorrel's nostrils flared. It bobbed its head, a sure sign that it sensed something was amiss. Davy probed every shadow. His thumb curling around Liz's hammer, he rode between a pair of high trees. Through a break in the growth the base of the hill was visible. Not a living soul was present.

"We're too late," Davy whispered to the maiden, turning his head to do so. A shadow fell across his face, a shadow he mistook for the flight of a bird until he glanced at the branches overhead.

Three painted Fox warriors armed with war clubs had launched themselves from their perches. Fierce yells tearing from their throats, they hurtled downward.

Chapter Three

Flavius Harris had died. He was sure of it. So when he heaved up out of a dark pit into the bright light of the Hereafter, he did not open his eyes right away. Instead, he lay still, perplexed by a gentle rocking movement. In a while he concluded that he must be floating on a cloud.

It was perfectly natural for a spirit, wasn't it?

Flavius keyed his ears to a peculiar swishing sound repeated over and over. He did not hear any harp music, which Matilda swore was the favorite of angels and cherubs. What he did hear, though, moments later, was a loud grunt. It disturbed him greatly. He did not know a lot about Heaven, but he was sure that grunting, like belching and passing wind, would hardly be allowed.

Maybe he was not where he thought he was.

Maybe he had gone *down* rather than up.

Homecoming

Someone spoke in a guttural tone that sounded a lot like an Indian tongue. It confirmed his fear. Hadn't his own parson asserted that all heathens were bound for the fiery depths, not the pearly gates?

Lord Almighty, spare me! Flavius thought, then realized to his horror that he had uttered the words aloud. The swishing ceased. The rocking motion slowed. Something nudged his leg, but he ignored it.

As a child, Flavius had frequently been hauled out to the woodshed by his pa and tanned severely for misbehaving. After each licking, he'd always felt like curling into a ball and bawling his brains out. He felt the same way now.

Again something nudged him. The same voice spoke, and he knew the speaker was addressing him. "Go away and leave me be," Flavius said. "I want to suffer in peace, consarn it."

A hard jab to the gut was impossible to ignore. Speared by pain, Flavius snapped up into a sitting posture and opened his eyes. He would be damned if he was going to lie there and let a demon torment him!

The first sight Flavius saw was the bright blue vault of sky speckled by fluffy white clouds. He was seated in a long canoe, water flowing gently on either side. Before him stood a stocky, short Indian dressed in a loincloth and little else. Behind Flavius was another.

There were no hellish flames. There was no brimstone, no sulphurous stench. He had not died, after all. But he might wish that he had before too long, depending on what his captors intended to do.

The man in the bow flung words at him that were so much gibberish. Shaking his head to show that he did not comprehend, Flavius smiled and held his

33

hands palm outward. "Friend!" he declared, repeating it in the Creek and the Seminole tongues on the off chance the pair might understand. Their blank expressions were proof they did not.

The Indians were not from any tribe Flavius had ever encountered. They were finely muscled, but not in the bulging kind of way that, say, a blacksmith would be. Their tawny skins reminded him of healthy cougars. They had dark eyes, white teeth. Black hair swept back from their foreheads. The man in front wore a red ornament in his hair, held in place by a thick needle-like clip. Their buckskin loincloths covered more of their backsides than their fronts.

Like the warriors, their canoe was unlike any Flavius had beheld. It was high at both ends, which was very unusual. The skin had been made from birch, the frame of cedar. The paddles, however, as well as the thwarts that held the gunwales together, had been fashioned of hard maple. All in all, it was an outstanding craft, finely detailed, precisely constructed.

The Indians exchanged comments. Flavius had not given much thought to his personal effects until he glanced again over his shoulder at the second warrior. There, in a small pile, were his pistols, rifle, powder horn, ammo pouch, knife, and possibles bag. In short, everything that meant anything to him.

He was tempted to try to grab the pistols. But both warriors sported long knives in deerskin sheaths. The four-foot paddles in their hands would also be formidable weapons if wielded as clubs. He opted to wait until a better chance came along.

Of the dun, there was no sign. Flavius doubted that the Indians had killed it. They'd have no reason to other than to eat it, and so far as Flavius knew, the only tribe that ate horses was one he had heard of that lived far to the southwest, out beyond the Mississippi River in uncharted territory. The Apaches, they were called. He hadn't believed the frontiersman who'd told him, but Davy had confirmed it was true so it must be.

The man in the bow turned and commenced paddling. His broad shoulders powered each swing. The paddle hardly seemed to dip below the surface, yet the canoe shot forward as if fired from a cannon. It had to be remarkably light for it to glide as swiftly and easily as it did.

Flavius was glad to be alive. At the same time, he had a new worry, namely what the Indians would do to him once they got him to their village. Quite a few tribes tortured their enemies. Not out of any perverse desire to see others suffer. No, they inflicted torture as a means of gauging the courage of their captives.

The Hurons, for example, once tortured an Iroquois by burning small parts of his body at a time. The man endured the torment for almost twelve hours before he gave up the ghost. Then he was cut into small pieces which were passed around for the Hurons to eat in tribute to his bravery.

The memory made Flavius queasy. He'd much rather that his captors did him in quickly. If not, his only consolation was that no other whites would witness his screaming and pleading.

Flavius was not about to deceive himself. He wasn't the most courageous of men, and his threshold for pain was very low. It wouldn't take much to reduce him to a pathetic wreck.

The stream they were on joined another, which in turn was linked to a third. High reeds and wild grass flanked them most of the time.

Flavius's head hurt, and there was a knot where the dun had kicked him. He needed to rest, but he forced himself to stay awake. His life depended on getting his hands on his guns. Eventually the Indians were bound to make a mistake.

Mile after mile fell behind them, however, and the pair never let down their guard. Only once did they stop, so the man in the bow could go off into some trees. The warrior behind Flavius kept a hand on the hilt of his knife the whole time.

The sun was on its downward arc when the canoe swept around a bend. Before them appeared a large island dotted by trees. Flavius looked up and his heart sank. He would never have an opportunity to get away now.

A large village had been established on the island. Odd dome-shaped wigwams outnumbered the trees. Wisps of smoke curled from cooking fires. Adults and children were everywhere, some of the former taking their leisure, some busy at various tasks. Canoes similar to the one in which Flavius rode lined the shore.

The man in the bow stood, tilted his head, and yipped long and loud. It drew dozens to the water's edge to greet the newcomers.

Flavius wanted to crawl into his own skin and hide. He was doomed. He just knew it. He'd never see Matilda again, never savor one of her intimate cuddles. It wouldn't surprise him if he wound up like that Iroquois, and he could only hope that all those who ate pieces of him became as sick as dogs. It would serve them right.

The Indians were chatting gaily until the canoe coasted to rest. Silence descended as each and every one regarded Flavius so intently that his skin prickled with gooseflesh. He was half afraid to twitch for fear of being riddled with arrows.

A commotion at the rear of the crowd heralded the arrival of a tall warrior dressed in exquisite buckskins, including a coat adorned with weasel tails and woven beadwork that must have taken months to make. A fur headband crowned his mane of hair, which was tinged with gray. In his right hand he clasped a ball-headed war club, the ball crafted from metal, not wood as Flavius would have expected.

The deference paid the tall man marked him as a tribal leader. Stalking to the canoe, he pointed the war club at Flavius and uttered a stern pronouncement. The next moment the warriors swarmed forward.

Davy Crockett slapped his legs against his sorrel as the three Fox warriors plummeted toward him. The horse had barely taken a stride when the men were on him. He brought up his rifle too late. A heavy body rammed into his shoulder and sent him sailing.

Wawaneechotinka cried out, but there was nothing Davy could do for her. He had his own hands full. As he crashed to earth, he rolled onto his knees. Two of the warriors sprang, one grabbing Liz, the other pinning his arms so he could not defend himself. With a brutal heave, Davy wrenched free, but lost his rifle.

Pushing backward to gain room to move, Davy resorted to his pistols, drawing both. As he leveled them,

David Thompson

the vegetation around him parted, disgorging a dozen more swarthy figures who were on him in a twinkling. Under the press of numbers he was forced to the ground. Knees gouged his stomach, his legs. Iron hands wrapped around his arms.

One of them jostled Davy's left hand. His finger involuntarily tightened on the trigger and the flintlock went off. Several of the warriors jumped back. For a few seconds his left arm was loose, and he bashed it across the temple of a hefty Fox holding his right arm. The man sagged.

Davy sought to take advantage by jerking his right arm free, but the warriors had others ideas. Recovering, they closed in, so many covering him that he could not lift a finger, let alone shoot. The pistols were pried from his grasp. His knife was taken. So was his tomahawk.

Only when all his weapons were removed did the warriors rise and step away from him. Davy slowly sat up. War clubs, arrows, and cold steel ringed him. His coonskin cap had fallen, so he picked it up, careful not to make any sudden moves.

Two brawny men held the maiden. She kicked at their shins, even tried to bite one of them. Her resistance faded when a new man strode onto the scene. Blanching, she stiffened and recoiled as if confronted by a viper. "Kiyo Kaga!" she spat.

The fox leader was an imposing specimen. Wide shoulders surmounted a bearish frame. His features were harsh to the point of being cruel. Red paint on his cheeks and temples accented his fierce aspect, as did the strip of hair down the middle of his head, which jutted upward like the sharp quills of a porcupine. He carried himself with an arrogant swagger. In his left hand was a long lance, the tempered blade over a foot and a half long. Eagle feathers and strips of fur decorated it.

Kiyo Kaga marched up to Wawaneechotinka and sneered. Fixing his mocking smile on Crockett, he came over and examined Davy much as he might a new type of insect. He fingered the coonskin cap, and made a remark that brought laughter from a few of his followers.

A warrior had caught hold of the sorrel's reins and was leading the skittish animal back. The horse did not like being handled by someone it did not know, so it was giving the warrior a hard time. Nickering nervously, it tugged and stomped.

Kiyo Kaga stared at the animal a few moments, then elevated his lance.

"No!" Davy hollered, flinging himself at the chief's legs. A blow to the chest brought him up short and he collapsed in anguish, his ribs aflame. He was surrounded and heaved erect.

The leader hefted the lance but did not hurl it. Growling at several men, he gestured and hiked southward.

Leather thongs were slipped over Davy's wrists, binding them. Another went around his neck. Like a dog on a leash he was led by a Fox who took sadistic delight in yanking on the cord every now and then, even though Davy did not flag. Behind him trudged Wawaneechotinka, the perfect picture of dejection. Her wrists were also tied, but she was spared the indignity of the leash.

A feeling of helplessness crept over Davy, but he

shrugged it off and set his mind to work devising a way out of his predicament.

Not being a quitter stemmed in large part from the influence of his pa. John Crockett had been a frontier ranger during the Revolutionary War. Afterward, he took to farming and scraped to feed his growing family. They never exactly prospered, but they never starved either.

In all, Davy's father and mother brought nine children into the world, six boys and three girls. Davy was the fifth of the boys. By the time he came along, there were so many mouths to feed that all the children toiled from dawn to dusk, helping out as best they were able.

Never once did John Crockett complain. Never once did he let hardship break him. "A man does what has to be done, come what may," he often told Davy. "In this world of ours, it's root hog or die. Never forget that."

Davy hadn't.

So now, unarmed and hogtied, flanked by cold-faced Fox warriors, he contemplated how best to save his hide and that of the lovely Chippewa.

The warriors were too watchful for him to simply bolt, nor would he even if he could if it meant leaving the maiden behind.

Brute force was out of the question. There were too blamed many hostiles. Even if by some miracle he got his hands on his guns, they would cut him down after he dropped two or three.

There was but one way out that Davy could see.

Talking his way out of scrapes was second nature to Davy, so much so that he preferred it to resorting to his fists to settle disputes. He had a gift for gab, a flair with words few could rival. When he put his mind to it, he could outtalk practically anyone, tangling them in a verbal web that left them at his mercy.

Suddenly the Fox warrior holding the leash gave another tug. Davy nearly tripped over his own feet. The warrior chortled.

Davy squared his shoulders and hiked on. It was time to let his wits be his guide. Adopting a casual air, he smiled at his tormentor and began to whistle. It was almost comical the way the warrior abruptly halted and gazed at him in blatant bewilderment. Soon every last Fox was staring at him with the same look. Except for one.

Kiyo Kaga's stern visage never changed. He studied Davy a moment, then snapped commands. The column resumed its march.

Davy continued to whistle, pretending he did not have a care in the world. It was his opening ploy in a gambit that would either bring about his release or end in a terrible death. With the stakes so high, he whistled louder.

Chapter Four

It was his worst nightmare made real.

First the dogs came sniffing around, growling and snapping if he so much as lifted a finger. Next it was the small children. Little girls who giggled and shyly spied on him from behind the lodges. Little boys who tossed dirt in his face or pelted him with rocks.

An old woman was worse. She walked past him five or six times during the afternoon, and in each instance she struck him with a gnarled walking stick.

Flavius Harris was bruised and sore and mightily famished by sunset. The sole encouraging note was that he had not been slain. Yet.

He had tried to communicate with his captors, to no avail. Who they were remained as much as a mystery as what they planned to do. Shortly before the sun went down, many of the men entered the largest wigwam in the village. For a council, Flavius reasoned, to determine his fate.

The Indians had secured him with a rope to a five-foot post they'd imbedded in the center of the village. The rope was tied to his right ankle and long enough to allow him limited movement. At first he had thought it strange that they neglected to bind his hands. Then it dawned on him that they did not need to.

Slipping out of the village without being spotted would be next to impossible. Even if he did it, where would he go? He was on an island in the middle of nowhere. They would catch him in no time.

Glumly, Flavius sat and contemplated the large lodge, hoping against hope that the Indians would decide to let him live. Or that Davy would come along soon and rescue him.

Flavius had a lot of faith in his friend. It was based on more than the fact that Crockett was one of the most competent woodsmen in Tennessee. That Davy could track a turtle across an impassable bog or shoot out the eye of a squirrel at 200 yards was all well and good. But it was Davy's personality rather than his ability that inspired so much confidence.

Deep in his soul, Flavius knew that his friend would never desert him, no matter what. Crockett was as true as the day was long. It was said that if you made a friend of him, you had a friend for life, and Flavius believed it wholeheartedly.

A loyal friend, a formidable enemy. That was how someone had once described David Crockett, and Flavius felt it fit. He had a hunch that Davy was marked for great things. A while back he'd said as much. Naturally, Davy had laughed and joked that

Flavius had better stop swigging jugs so early in the morning.

Suddenly the flap covering the lodge entrance parted. Out came a warrior who hurried off into the darkness.

Disappointed, Flavius leaned against the pole. The patter of approaching footsteps did not register until a lean shape materialized beside him. He glanced up, and was taken back to behold the old woman with the walking stick. Figuring that she was there to brain him again, he ducked and covered his head with his arms, saying, "What did I ever do to you, you old crow? Leave me be, dadgum it!"

The woman snorted and said a few words. When he did not reply, she nudged his leg with her walking stick.

"Go away!" Flavius said. "Quit pestering me!" He peeked between his arms in anticipation of her blow, but she merely stood there staring at him as if he were a mad dog she'd very much like to put out of its misery.

The old woman shook the stick at him, then held out her other hand. In it was a birch-bark bowl filled with a steamy mass.

"You done brought me food?" Flavius declared, shocked. Bracing himself in case it was a trick to get him to lower his guard, he tentatively accepted the bowl. She nodded curtly before stalking away to her dwelling.

No fork or spoon had been provided, but Flavius did not care. He was hungry enough to eat live caterpillars. Dipping his fingers into the mash, he ladled it into his mouth. Whatever it was, it was delicious. He rolled it on his tongue, savoring the taste. Mainly it consisted of wild rice and onions, with some kind of seasoning added.

Flavius downed every last bit. When he was done, he licked the bowl. Twice. Momentarily content, he rested with the bowl cradled in his lap, wishing the old crow would bring him more. He closed his eyes and dozed.

A jab on his leg brought him around. Flavius straightened, assuming the woman was back. "I'd like a second—" he began, but turned to stone when he saw the three warriors who ringed him.

One untied his ankle. At spear point he was prodded toward the large lodge. In his anxiety he held onto the bowl until a warrior noticed and plucked it from his grasp. He had to stoop to enter, and immediately was racked by a fit of intense coughing thanks to heavy smoke that choked the lodge from shoulder height to the ventilation hole at the top.

Twenty bronzed faces were cast toward him. Twenty inscrutable faces that gave him no clue as to what they were thinking.

"Howdy," Flavius bleated, mustering a sickly smile. Somehow he had to get it across to his captors that he was friendly. Maybe then they would go easy on him.

At the head of the lodge sat the tall leader with the fur headband. He beckoned, and Flavius was steered between the two rows and forced to kneel in front of him.

The chief scrutinized the backwoodsman, then touched his own chest and said, "Keekweechiweepinank." He looked at Flavius as if expecting an answer.

Flavius's mind raced. He was at a loss to know what to say. Their tongue was as foreign as Russian would be. Had the leader asked him a question? Or made a comment? What was he supposed to do?

Rather impatiently, the chief again touched himself. "Keekweechiweepinank," he repeated, and pointed at Flavius.

An older warrior who sat on the leader's right leaned forward, placing his palm on his sternum, and said, "Kawakatusk." He too pointed at Flavius, his bushy eyebrows arching.

In a blaze of understanding, Flavius grinned and tapped his own torso. "Flavius Augustus Harris," he proclaimed. If they had been white men, he would have gone on to explain that his pa had attended a highfalutin school in Philadelphia as a boy and picked up a smattering of Latin. Ever since, his pa liked to show off by using Latin every chance he got.

The Indians would never understand.

Flavius waited nervously as they talked amongst themselves. When Keekweechiweepinank raised a hand, silence fell. The chief's dark eyes bored into his.

"Why you come our country?"

Flabbergasted, Flavius blinked and half rose. A firm hand shoved him back in place. "You speak our tongue?" he exclaimed. "Why didn't you say so sooner? We could have cleared up this whole affair and I could have been on my way."

"Why come?" Keekweechiweepinank repeated. "Not many whites come. Man in long dress. Trappers once. But that be all."

Immensely heartened, Flavius said, "My friend and I are from the sovereign state of Tennessee. We're on

46

a gallivant to see what we can see, and we sure as blazes don't mean you or your kin any harm. We're just passing through, is all."

The chief placed a hand on the war club at his side. "You not come steal women?"

Flavius chuckled. "Whatever would we do that for when we both have wives back at home? Why, if I so much as looked crosswise at another woman, Matilda would take a shovel to my noggin." He shook his head. "No, sir. We are not on the scout for females."

Keekweechiweepinank pondered awhile. When Kawakatusk addressed him, he nodded and said in English, "Maybe you speak with two tongues, white man. Maybe you think we fools."

"Why would I lie?" Flavius said defensively. "Ask the warriors who found me. I had no female with me. I was nowhere near your village. Anyone who claims I came to steal your womenfolk is the one speaking with two tongues."

The leader gestured. At a word from a warrior near the entrance, the flap opened and in came an old woman. Flavius gaped. It was the scrawny wildcat he had saved from the war party. Inadvertently, he pressed his fingers to the scratch marks she had left on his cheeks.

"You know Tokawonda?" Keekweechiweepinank asked stiffly.

"Not by name, but we've met," Flavius said. "She and a pretty young thing were jumped by a war party. Davy—that's my partner—grabbed the pretty gal and left the hag to me."

"Hag?" the chief said.

Flavius bobbed his head at the old woman, who

stood demurely to one side. Smirking, he said, "That's what we call females who are long in the tooth and as mean as a stuck snake." He winked at the leader. "You must know the kind I mean."

Keekweechiweepinank did not so much as crack a grin. "Tokawonda is my mother."

An icy chill pierced Flavius. "Your ma?" he croaked. "Hey, I didn't mean anything by that crack I made. It was a joke. Your people must poke fun at each other all the time."

"Ojibwas never say bad things about Ojibwas," Keekweechiweepinank said severely. "As for pretty young thing," he quoted exactly, "she is Wawaneecho-tinka, my sister."

"Oh, God," Flavius said under his breath. How could he have been so dumb? He had gone and insulted the head man's flesh and blood! To ease the sting, he said quickly, "Ask your ma. She'll tell you that Davy and me were trying to help them, not steal them. It was those other Indians who were up to no good."

"If this be true, where is your friend? Where is my sister?" Keekweechiweepinank placed the war club in front of him. "Maybe friend and you think to steal women for your own. Maybe that be why you take them from Fox warriors."

Flavius was so incensed by the accusation that his temper flared. Stabbing a finger at the chief's mother, he snapped, "Want *her?* I'd have to be as blind as a bat and as randy as an elk in rut! She's old enough to be my grandma, for crying out loud!"

A hardening of Keekweechiweepinank's features warned Flavius that he had gone too far. Other warriors shared their leader's outrage, and shifted as if eager to spring on him. A lump formed in his throat. He had to cough to clear it, then said contritely, "Not that I meant she isn't a fine woman. I'm sure she is in her own right. But she's just not the type I'd be likely to steal. I'm more partial to pretty young things."

Even as Flavius said it, he knew that he had made another dreadful mistake. He had not only stuffed his foot in his mouth, but his leg clear to the hipbone.

"Pretty young thing," Keekweechiweepinank said. "Like my sister."

"No, no, no," Flavius said. "I wouldn't steal her either. Neither would Davy. We're *married*, darn it. It wouldn't be right for us to dally with strange womenfolk."

"I do not believe you, white man," Keekweechiweepinank said bluntly. "I think your friend stole Wawaneechotinka. I think you should die."

Murmuring erupted along both rows. Flavius squirmed, resisting a mad impulse to bolt. He would not get three feet. "We're innocent, I tell you!" he hollered. "We were trying to help your women, not take them captive."

The murmuring grew louder. It was not terribly difficult for Flavius to assess the mood of those assembled. There had to be something he could say or do that would show them the error of their ways, but for the life of him he could not think of what it was.

At that juncture the gray-haired warrior, Kawakatusk, rose and made a short speech. The others listened attentively. Evidently his counsel held weight, for when he was done the rest discussed whatever he had told them for quite some time. At last their leader focused on Flavius.

"You say your friend try to help. You say he not keep Wawaneechotinka. I not believe you. But Kawakatusk think we must be fair. We give friend chance to prove your words true."

Sheer, ecstatic relief filled Flavius to the brim. "How can he prove it?" he asked, his vocal cords unusually raspy.

"If friend do as you claim, him bring sister soon," Keekweechiweepinank said. "If not, that mean you speak with two tongues."

Flavius wanted to shout for joy. Davy would not let him down. Sooner or later the pair would show up. "How much time are you willing to give him?"

"If Wawaneechotinka not back in three sleeps," Keekweechiweepinank said, and swung his war club as if he were bashing in the cranium of a foe, "you die by my hand."

"Can't you give him a little more than that?" Flavius said. Three days should be more than enough, but there was no telling what Davy might run into along the way. Any delay, and *he* was the one who would pay the price. "Why not seven sleeps? Or fourteen? Or a full moon?"

"Three sleeps," Keekweechiweepinank repeated.

Kawakatusk was smiling at Flavius. He realized he should be grateful for the venerable warrior's intervention, but he was too distressed to do more than nod in response as the same three men who had brought him to the council lodge heaved him to his feet and hauled him outside. The cool air was invigorating after the stifling, smoky interior.

The Ojibwas tied him to the post. One kicked dirt on him as they departed.

Homecoming

Flavius endured the abuse without complaint. His mouth had already gotten him into enough hot water. It would be foolhardy to provoke them any further.

Left alone, Flavius slumped and lamented his fate. He never should have gone off with Davy. Matilda had warned him not to. She'd flat out told him that it was senseless for a grown man to be wandering from Dan to Beersheba when he had a wife and sprouts to look after.

For once Flavius had stood up to her. Not out of ill will, or because he was sick of her companionship. He'd simply wanted to roam a bit, to take in the sights. He'd not gone off to fight the Creeks as Davy had done. Truth was, he'd never strayed more than seventy-five miles from the place where he was born. It was high time he saw something of the world, he'd thought.

So curiosity was to blame. And everyone knew what curiosity had done to the proverbial cat.

Flavius lifted apprehensive eyes to the heavens. Unless his friend appeared within three days, his life was over. Davy where are you? he mentally screamed.

Of course there was no answer.

Davy Crockett did not like being trussed up like a hog for slaughter. He lay on his left side twenty feet from a crackling fire, ignored by his captors. They had not bothered to feed him, had not even offered him anything to drink.

Shortly before the sun sank, Kiyo Kaga had called a halt in a clearing. Some of the warriors had gone off to hunt, others to collect firewood. A doe had served as their evening meal. The tantalizing aroma had had

51

Davy's stomach growling and grumbling for over an hour.

Now and then one of the Fox men had come over and checked his bonds. The rest of the time it was as if he did not exist.

Wawaneechotinka was another story. Kiyo Kaga had forced her to sit next to him at the fire. She'd been given water, which she'd accepted, then offered a portion of roasted meat, which she'd refused. The Fox leader, so considerate and polite to her until then, had turned on her, seizing her wrist and twisting it until she began eating as he wanted. As soon as she'd taken a bite, Kiyo Kaga had oozed snakish charm again.

Davy had never been much of a hater, but he found himself growing to despise Kiyo Kaga as he had few others. The man had an obvious cruel streak. It was clear, also, that Kiyo Kaga had his sights set on the maiden. Davy felt sorry for her. When the time was ripe, Kiyo Kaga was going to force himself on Wawaneechotinka, then as likely as not cast her aside like yesterday's garbage.

Unless Davy could get them out of there. He glanced at his sorrel, tethered in a patch of grass south of the campfire. The saddle had not been removed. A couple of warriors had tugged at the cinch, but had never gotten the hang of undoing it.

As for Davy's personal effects, they had been distributed among the band. Kiyo Kaga had his rifle, another warrior had his pistols, a third his knife, and so on. Reclaiming them posed a problem, but he would not leave without them. His hunting tools, as he liked to call them, were as necessary to his survival as his arms and legs.

Homecoming

Davy pretended to drift off while spying on the Foxes through slitted eyelids. One by one they turned in, the last doing so shortly before midnight. Wawa-neechotinka was given a blanket and permitted to lie by herself on the opposite side of the fire. Kiyo Kaga stretched out near her.

A lone man was left on guard. Armed with a bow that he carried slung over his left shoulder, he got up every so often to patrol the clearing.

Davy set to work on freeing his hands. By rubbing his wrists constantly back and forth, he gradually loosened the cord. It was painful work. His skin was scraped raw and bled slightly, but that did not deter him from renewing his effort whenever the guard's back was to him.

It was past two in the morning when Davy's wrists grew slippery enough to slide them out of the stretched loops. Prudently keeping his arms close together so the sentry would not notice, he turned as if tossing in his sleep, contriving to bend so his hands were close to his ankles.

The knots were as tight as closed clams. Davy pried and pried, breaking a fingernail in the process. He succeeded in picking apart the first, and started on the second.

So intent was he on his bonds that he had not paid any attention to the guard for quite a while. The scrape of a moccasin on grass alerted him to his oversight. Breathing heavily to give the impression he was deep in slumber, Davy peered past his feet and saw the sentry warily stalking toward him.

The man suspected something was wrong. He had

David Thompson

partially drawn a long knife and moved in a sideways crouch.

Davy feigned a soft snore. The warrior stopped and observed the rise and fall of his chest. He must have been convincing because, ever so slowly, the knife was replaced. Straightening, the Indian moseyed over to the fire and hunkered down to add more dead branches.

Davy resumed his assault on the last knot. He did not care that his fingers hurt like the dickens. He did not care that the flesh under the broken nail was bleeding. Pulling and plucking, he parted the stubborn cord. Both ends fell onto the grass.

The warrior was holding his hands to the fire to warm them. He tossed his head to fight off drowsiness, then yawned.

Silently pushing to his feet, Davy moved among the sleeping men. He came to the one who had taken his tomahawk. It was beside the man, the handle propped across a thick war club. Davy's fingers wrapped around it just as the warrior grunted and rolled over, facing him.

Chapter Five

Davy Crockett was determined not to be captured a second time. If the warrior woke up, he planned to grab Wawaneechotinka and dash into the forest. He would probably have to fight his way through, but it could not be helped. Once there, they might elude the Fox band.

The sleeper stirred, but did not open his eyes. In seconds he was sleeping peacefully. He did not utter a sound when Davy rose.

The man by the fire was fiddling with a stick, poking it into the flames so it would catch fire and then extinguishing it with a few puffs of breath.

Davy stepped over another sleeper, circled a third. The one who had claimed his pistols had placed them in a parfleche and deposited the bag on a stump. Davy sank onto a knee, slipped his hand under the flap, and removed the flintlocks one at a time. He wedged them under his belt.

Off in the woods an owl hooted. The guard idly lifted his head to gaze in its direction, which just happened to be in the same direction as the stump.

Davy flattened, pressing his body against the ground, heedless of a stone that gouged his leg. The stump was barely high enough to screen him. If the warrior looked closely, the jig was up.

But the man only scanned the woods and went back to playing with the stick.

Davy let some time go by before he crawled into the open. The Fox who had appropriated his butcher knife was dangerously close to the fire. Once there, Davy would be bathed in the full glare of the firelight. He would have nowhere to hide. Should the sentry turn, all hell would bust loose.

The knife hung by a leather cord from the Indian's right shoulder. Since the man now lay on his left side, the knife and sheath were on the ground in front of him. Davy had to get within a few inches of the Fox in order to retrieve his weapon.

Trying to untie the cord or to slip it over the man's head was bound to wake him up. Davy relied on the keen edge of his tomahawk. Placing it on top of the cord near the sheath, he applied his full weight to the handle. The tomahawk sheared the thin leather as handily as a hot table knife would shear through butter. He added his butcher knife to the growing collection tucked under his belt.

That left his long rifle, powder horn, ammo pouch, and a small bag in which he kept personal effects. Kiyo Kaga had them all.

Homecoming

The man by the fire tossed the stick into the flames, then stretched. He gazed at the stars, evidently noting the position of the Big Dipper.

It might be a sign that the warrior was getting set to wake up another man to relieve him. Davy did not want that to happen. The new sentry would be more alert and bound to check on their prisoner first thing.

Changing his grip on the tomahawk, Davy crept up behind the guard. Each foot he raised and set down as carefully as if he were walking on broken glass. An arm's length away he paused to hike the tomahawk on high. A glance confirmed that none of the sleepers had moved.

The sentry stretched again, placed his hands flat, and began to push himself up off the ground.

Throwing all the strength in his shoulders and upper arms into a lightning swing, Davy brought the flat side of the tomahawk down on the warrior's noggin. There was a thud and the man collapsed like a poled ox. Davy had to seize hold of the sentry's shoulders to keep him from pitching into the fire.

Another hasty glance showed that the thud had not been loud enough to rouse anyone.

Davy slowly lowered the heavy frame. Other than a nasty bump and an awful headache, the man would wake up in the morning no worse for wear.

Davy could have killed the Fox, but he was not one of those frontiersmen who believed that the only good Indians were dead ones. Besides which, he'd had his full of slaughter during the Creek War. If he could help it, he never killed unless his life or that of someone else was in immediate peril.

He might make an exception tonight, though.

Kiyo Kaga was a mighty tempting target. Davy stood over him, debating what to do. From what Wa-waneechotinka had said and what he had seen, the man was as cruel as they came. It was Kiyo Kaga who was to blame for the latest flare-up of hostilities between the Ojibwas and the Fox tribe. Should he die, the hostilities might cease. Countless lives would be spared.

Cocking his arm, Davy prepared to strike. Seconds elapsed, and still the tomahawk hung suspended in the air. Frowning, Davy lowered it. He just couldn't bring himself to slay someone who was powerless to resist, even if that person deserved to be rubbed out.

But there was hope yet. Kiyo Kaga might awaken and try to stop him, in which case he would be entirely justified in splitting the chief's head like an overripe melon.

Davy's powder horn, bullet pouch, and possibles bag were piled close at hand. Davy slung each across his chest. The rifle posed a problem in that Kiyo Kaga had one brawny hand wrapped around the barrel. Grasping the stock, Davy tried to ease Liz loose. The chief clung on, mumbling in his sleep.

A whisper of movement forewarned Davy that his luck had run out. He made a stab for a pistol, checking his draw when he saw that it was Wawaneechotinka who had sat up, not one of the warriors. Shrugging out of the blanket, she rose onto her knees and extended her bound wrists.

Motioning, Davy indicated that he would help her in a moment. He was not giving up on Liz. Bending, he lightly brushed the tomahawk's handle across the back of Kiyo Kaga's hand. Kiyo Kaga shifted, exhaling loudly. When his breathing returned to normal, Davy tried once more.

The trick worked when his wife was snoring. Many a night he had been roused out of a pleasant dream by her sawing logs. Being a gentleman, he'd never awakened her or mentioned it to her the next day. He'd coped either by gently bouncing up and down on the mattress until she quieted, or by lightly touching her until she changed position, at which point the snoring always stopped.

A third time Davy rubbed the handle across the Fox leader's hand. Kiyo Kaga seemed to stop breathing altogether, and for a moment Davy thought he would wake up. But then Kiyo Kaga rolled over, away from him, releasing the Kentucky.

Davy felt like a whole man again as he scooted to the maiden and swiftly slashed the cords binding her. To his consternation, she flung herself into his arms and pressed warm lips to his cheek. He smiled, then took her hand and headed for the sorrel. Once they were on it, there was no stopping them. Davy would have her back with her own people in short order and then go find Flavius.

They passed several sleepers, and had only one man to go by when the sorrel saw them coming and whinnied. The man promptly sat up, rubbing his eyes to clear them.

Davy swept the rifle in a smooth arc, but he was too slow by half. The warrior spied them and let out with a shriek that would have done justice to a banshee. The stock caught him above the ear and down he went just as other warriors leaped to their feet.

It would take too long to reach the horse, untie it,

and climb on with Wawaneechotinka. Davy had no recourse but to grip her wrist and sprint for the trees. Angry shouts were flung at them. A zinging arrow missed him by inches as the foliage closed around them.

It was safe to say that Kiyo Kaga was fit to be tied. His bellows thundered above the confusion, whipping his warriors into pursuit.

"He say to kill you," Wawaneechotinka translated.

Davy veered to the left, circling the clearing instead of making a beeline deep into the forest as the Fox men were likely to figure he would. A new ruckus broke out, and he glanced between some trees to see his sorrel rearing high, its front hooves flailing. The uproar had spooked the horse and it wanted to get out of there. Warriors were trying to stop it, but the tether had snapped and they could not snatch the reins or the bridle. A flying hoof slammed one man in the chest and he went down like a broken doll.

Kiyo Kaga roared instructions, gesturing savagely at the sorrel.

A lean warrior with a lance tried to slip in close, and received a kick to the collarbone that broke it with a distinct crack. Howling, the man flopped on the grass, clutching his injury.

Davy owed that horse a debt he could never repay. It had bought them the precious moments needed to effect their escape. He ran on, staying shy of openings until he was on the opposite side of the clearing from where he had plunged into the woods.

The sorrel had knocked another man down and was wheeling. Three members of the band lunged, but they could not prevent the animal from galloping into the darkness.

Kiyo Kaga was positively livid, his face so red it looked as if he were about to explode. Shoving men to the right and left, he ordered them into the woods.

Davy wished that the sorrel had run toward him instead of to the southeast. Nodding at Wawaneechotinka, he bent their steps northward, jogging until he had an ache in his side and could not travel another yard. The maiden kept up every step of the way, and never once griped about the pace he maintained.

By his estimation they were over a mile from the clearing. He leaned against a trunk, hands on his knees, sucking air into his lungs. All things considered, it had not turned out too badly. He'd lost his horse, but he still had his tools and rifle and—best of all—his hair.

Wawaneechotinka stepped up to him and tenderly stroked his cheek. "Thank you, Red Cheeks, for saving me."

Davy grinned. "No need to make a fuss. It's what knights in shining armor are supposed to do."

"Nights?" Wawaneechotinka said, and craned her neck to appraise the celestial spectacle above.

"Never mind," Davy said. He'd explain later, once they were safely in the clear. Straightening, he scoured their back trail, nearly jumping out of his skin when Wawaneechotinka molded her body against him and planted her mouth smack on his. Dumbfounded, he felt her velvet tongue trace the outline of his lips.

The maiden drew back, her eyes simmering coals.

"What was that for?" Davy asked, troubled that he

already knew. He had enough problems to deal with, without her waxing romantic.

"You be brave man," Wawaneechotinka said. "Good man." Her finger found his ear and tweaked the lobe. "Kind of man I like. Kind of man I want."

"Hold your horses," Davy said, peeling loose before she did something they would both regret. "I have a wife. My second. Her name is Elizabeth Parton, and I took a vow to be true to her all my born days."

Davy assumed that would settle it. The maiden would let well enough be and he could get on with the business of taking her to her people. He should have known better. Where women were concerned, nothing could be taken for granted. They were as unpredictable as tornadoes, as mysterious as the Northern Lights.

Wawaneechotinka draped her slender arms over his shoulders and swayed her hips in an enticing manner. "Your home is many sleeps from here. Why go back? Why not stay?"

"Land sakes alive!" Davy said. This was a new experience. He'd never been one of those men who had to beat women off with a club. More often than not his interest in particular women had been one-sided. Polly, his first wife, had not taken a shine to him until after a long courtship. Elizabeth had been more receptive, but secretly he suspected that her being a widow with two kids of her own had had more to do with it than his looks.

"I make you happy," Wawaneechotinka was saying. "I give you many children."

Just what Davy needed. Counting Elizabeth's, he had six to provide for as it was. To buy time he said,

Homecoming

"This isn't hardly the best place to talk about your feelings. Let's discuss it later, once we're safe, shall we?"

To forestall her answer, Davy hastened northward. He'd wanted to rest a while longer, but under the circumstances he was willing to sacrifice.

Judging by the sky, dawn would come in two and a half hours. That should give them a substantial lead, since Davy had every confidence the Fox war party would not find their trail before first light, if then.

The north woods were serenely quiet, broken by the occasional grunt of a roving bear or the rarer screams of big cats. A chill breeze out of the northwest fanned the leaves.

Davy was not the least bit afraid. The forest was his home. He had been born and bred in the backwoods, and was more at ease there than he would be in a city or town. The habits of every creature were like an open book. Its plants and trees were old friends.

Since he had worn three-cornered pants, nature had always fascinated him. Some of his earliest memories were of going on "nature strolls" with his pa, who took him to a local pond so he could watch the turtles, frogs, and fish. Another was of an old maple tree out back of his pa's cabin, a tree he clambered over from top to bottom and got to know as well as he knew the back of his own hand.

One of Davy's most vivid memories was his first encounter with a bear. He'd been three years old at the time, or so his folks later told him. So young, yet it was indelibly branded in his mind.

He had been out back of the cabin playing in some dirt when an enormous black beast had ambled out of the woods. To his childish eyes the bear had been a huge, hairy cow, but a cow with tapered teeth, revealed when it sniffed at the dirt and sneezed.

Strange to say, Davy had not been afraid at all.

Not knowing what it was and thinking that it wanted to play, Davy had thrown a handful of dirt at it, and the bear had sneezed again. The sight of its muzzle and face sprinkled with earth had made him squeal in delight.

He had not known it at the time, but the squeal had brought his father to the back door. The next thing Davy knew, the bear's skull had exploded in a shower of gore and blood, even as his mother was scooping him into her arms and whisking him into the cabin.

Davy remembered being taken out to see the dead bear later. Neighbors had been there, and his pa had been posing proudly with the trophy, saying that now the family would have enough meat to see them well into the winter. Davy had been praised for being so brave and facing the beast down.

It long bothered him. That old bear had been curious, not threatening. Sure, it might have gotten around to hurting him since bears were notoriously temperamental. But he always harbored the belief that his pa had been a mite hasty.

He never told anyone, but for years afterward he had a recurring dream in which the bear ambled out of the woods, knelt on its hind legs, and begged not to be killed. Every time he had the dream, he woke up in a cold sweat.

The last time he'd had it was a few days before he slew his first bear while on a hunt with his pa and uncle. Their dogs had treed a big she-bear and the two men had closed in to finish it off, leaving Davy where it would be safe.

Little had John Crockett realized that the she-bear had not been alone when the hounds gave chase. A two-year old cub, nearly full grown itself, had darted into a thicket and hidden until the four dogs went past. Shortly it emerged—and there was Davy, not twenty feet away.

Ordinarily, black bears would run from humans. This one had been frightened by the hounds and rattled by its narrow escape. So when it saw Davy, it must have thought that he was after it too. The bear did what any cornered bear would do; it rushed him.

How Davy got off a shot, he would never know. Everything happened so fast that he had fired and the bear was tumbling to rest almost at his feet before he quite knew what was going on. The shot had been made in pure reflex. Fortunately, by that age he'd spent many an hour target-shooting, practicing so long and hard that he was widely considered one of the best marksmen in the county despite his youth.

His pa had crowed like a rooster for weeks on end. Every customer who visited the tavern had had to endure the elder Crockett boasting how his boy had brought down "the fiercest bruin that ever lived" with a single shot through the brainpan.

After that the nightmares had ended. Why, Davy never could fathom. But he was powerful glad they did.

Suddenly a loud grunt off to the left brought an end to Davy's musing. Slowing, he surveyed the inky woods, and thought that he saw a bulky form flit from tree to tree.

"Bear," Wawaneechotinka whispered, sounding upset.

"Don't fret yourself," Davy said. "I've made rugs of more bears than I have fingers and toes."

"Silver-tips also, Red Cheeks?"

Davy's cockiness evaporated like dew under a blazing sun. Silver-tip was a white expression for the most feared bears alive, brutes so immense and so savage that even the most experienced mountain men avoided them. Another name for their breed was *grizzly*.

Unlike black bears, grizzlies had no fear of humans. Men and women were simply another kind of prey to them, and they stalked humans just as they would any other animal that had the misfortune of crossing their path when they were hungry.

Davy had never tangled with one himself. From the stories he'd heard, he didn't want to. A single shot rarely stopped a grizzly, not even a shot to the head, because a grizzly's skull was tremendously thick and sheathed by layers of compact muscle.

Now here he was, afoot in uncharted country in the middle of the night with a lovely woman to protect, and a grizzly had caught their scent!

Wawaneechotinka gripped Davy's arm so hard, it hurt. He put a finger to his lips and stood stock-still in the feeble hope that the bear would lose interest in them and wander off. But the moment he stopped, so did their mammoth shadow.

Davy could see the bear more clearly. It was as big as a bull, only wider across the shoulders, which were topped by a noticeable hump. The head was positively huge. It swung ponderously from side to side as the bear tested the wind.

"We must run!" Wawaneechotinka said.

"No!" Davy responded. Any woodsman worthy of the name knew that fleeing from a predator often triggered an attack. So far, the grizzly was keeping its distance, and Davy wanted to keep it that way.

Wawaneechotinka tugged on his arm, but Davy refused to budge. He was glad the wind was blowing from the bear to them or the grizzly might detect her fear. "Calm down," he advised. "We'll be all right so long as we don't panic."

The grizzly growled, then reared onto two legs. Davy swore that the creature was as tall as the trees. It was not the case, but it *seemed* that way. And the spectacle of a bear so gargantuan chilled the blood in his veins.

It was as if all the ghosts of all the bears he had slain over the years had combined into the unstoppable brute before him.

Davy tossed his head to dispel the nonsense he was thinking. The grizzly was made of flesh and blood and bone, just like every other bear. Like every other bear, it could be killed. He pointed Liz, but he did not fire. Only as a last resort would he let lead fly, since a wounded bear was three times as dangerous as one that was not.

Wawaneechotinka fidgeted like a stallion at a starting line. She still wanted to flee, and Davy did not blame her. His own legs were equally hard to control.

The bear might as well have been carved from stone. It neither moved nor made any sounds.

Davy's palms were sweating. A gust of wind increased the chill gnawing through him. He fingered the trigger, pondering whether to slowly back off while they still could. The hoot of an owl to the south did not merit any interest. Not until it was repeated, closer and louder, and his trained ears registered that the cry had not been made by a real owl but by an adept human mimic. An Indian. It had to be a Fox. Somehow, the war party was tracking them.

The grizzly also heard the cry, with an unforeseen result. Dropping onto all fours, the silver-tip shuffled toward them.

"Red Cheeks!" Wawaneechotinka gasped.

Davy stood so his body blocked hers. "I won't let it hurt you," he pledged.

"Not bear. There!"

Davy looked. The old saw about being between a rock and a hard place had never been more true. For swooping at them from out of the night was a pair of Fox warriors with upraised war clubs.

Chapter Six

When confronted by two evils, most men will pick the lesser.

Davy Crockett was no different. A choice between a colossal grizzly and a couple of warriors was no choice at all. No one in their right mind would go up against a grizzly, ever. He jammed his rifle to his shoulder and took a hasty bead on the foremost Fox.

The warriors did not slow, and it was just as well that they did not. From out of the undergrowth crashed the grizzly, plowing into the pair like a steam engine gone amok. A single swipe of a ham-sized paw decapitated the first warrior. His head flew end over end, spewing scarlet in its wake.

The second Fox attempted to spin, but the silver-tip was on him with the speed of thought. A scream tore from him as he was thrown to the earth. The grizzly's massive form hid him, but could not blot out his horrid screeches as teeth capable of crunching bone did so.

Davy was not one to look a gift horse in the mouth. Maybe the grizzly had seen the warriors as a menace to itself. Maybe it regarded them as competitors about to steal its rightful prey. Whatever the case, the Indians had saved the maiden and him from the bear and the bear had saved them from the Indians.

Another wavering screech tore from the warrior's throat as Davy sped off with Wawaneechotinka in tow. There was no need to spur her on. She fled as if demons from the pit of Hell were nipping at their heels.

Both of them knew that their lives still hung in the balance. The bear might finish with the Fox at any moment and come after them. And though enormous, the grizzly could speedily overtake them. Over short distances the great humpbacked bears were able to run as fast as horses.

Davy pumped his legs furiously. He lost track of which direction he was going. He simply ran, and ran, and ran. Limbs snatched at them. Rocks, logs, and roots tried to trip them. A branch jutting out of nowhere nearly poked out his eye. Yet he did not slow down until his companion started to have difficulty keeping up.

Wawaneechotinka was weaving unsteadily when Davy ducked behind a boulder the size of his sorrel, and hunkered down. His own breathing was ragged, his legs sore and wobbly. "I think we gave that varmint the slip," he rasped.

The maiden said something in her own tongue, then caught herself and repeated it in broken English. "Never know with—" and here she used the Ojibwa word for bear, or so Davy assumed. "If it still hungry, we be dead."

"I wish I may be shot if I ever give up without a fight," Davy responded. "Don't count us out until we're worm food. As my ma was partial to saying, where there's life, there's hope."

Her eyes the size of walnuts, Wawaneechotinka gazed fearfully into the murky forest. She shook from head to toe, then bit her lower lip and steadied herself.

Davy did not hold her fright against her. Only an idiot would take a grizzly lightly. Probably the only reason he wasn't scared to death was that he had hunted black bear many times in Tennessee and elsewhere. He didn't see a grizzly as some sort of indestructible behemoth, as many whites and red men were wont to do.

Wawaneechotinka sidled closer. Her shoulder brushed his, her breath caressed his face. "Again you save me, Red Cheeks," she whispered.

"All I did was run like hell," Davy noted. "It hardly makes me a hero."

"Hero?"

"Someone who does what has to be done even when the odds are stacked against him," Davy explained. Seeing that she did not quite comprehend, he added, "Someone who is brave where others might not be."

Wawaneechotinka placed her hand on his. "You are hero, Red Cheeks."

Davy did not like the sound of that. Here he was, just trying to do her a good turn, and she'd gone and fallen for him. Who would have thought it? Elizabeth would bust a gut laughing if she heard tell.

"There's something you'd better keep in mind,"

Davy said kindly. "As soon as I fetch you back to your kin, I'm leaving. Likely as not, we'll never see each other again."

"That make me sad," Wawaneechotinka confessed. "What if I find way you stay?"

"I can't," Davy emphasized. "Haven't you been listening to a word I've said? I have a wife and sprouts to get home to. It wouldn't hardly be right to up and desert them."

"You always do what be right?"

"I try mighty hard," Dave replied. "My pa used to say that a man should always be sure he's in the right, then go ahead and get done what needs doing. You could say I've lived by that motto all my life, and I reckon I'll go on living by it until the day I die."

Wawaneechotinka was going to say something, but a rumbling snort from the woods to their south transformed her into stone. Her nails bit into his hand again. She looked like a frightened fawn about to flee for its life.

So she should. The grizzly was stalking them. Davy rose and ran northward, making as little noise as he could, Wawaneechotinka in tow.

A grizzly's eyesight was poor compared to that of a hawk or eagle, its hearing no better than that of a mountain lion. But its sense of smell was exceptional, and that was how this particular beast was tracking them. So long as it did not actually spot them, it would take its sweet time.

Davy kept his eyes peeled for somewhere to make a stand or some way of eluding the brute. A stream would be ideal, but it was just their luck that they did not stumble on one. He contemplated giving Wawaneechotinka a boost into a high tree and following her up. Since grizzlies were too heavy to climb, they could wait the bear out. Eventually it would grow so famished that it would wander off, allowing them to effect their escape.

On the other hand, there had been instances where bears had treed someone and waited for days on end for their quarry to descend. Sometimes it became a contest to see which weakened first.

There was a story making the rounds that a few years back a trapper had been treed and grown so weak from lack of food and water that he had lashed himself to a limb so he would not fall. An account of his ordeal had been committed to a few scraps of paper he carried in his possibles bag. Over eighteen months later other trappers had found his skeleton, still strapped to the limb.

Davy did not want that to happen to the maiden and him. There had to be a better way than climbing a tree. But seek as he might, none presented themselves.

Hundreds of yards from the boulder, Davy paused to verify that the grizzly had not given up. The muted crack of a twig was all the proof he needed. Hastening on, he looped his free arm around Wawaneechotinka, who had taken to stumbling every half-dozen feet or so.

"Can you make it?" he whispered.

"I try."

"If the worst happens, I'll keep it busy as long as I can while you go on," Davy proposed. "Should you ever run into another white man, mention me to him and ask him to get word back to my family."

Surprisingly, Wawaneechotinka smiled. "Hero," she said.

Davy sighed. Maybe one day someone would explain to him why women only heard what they wanted to hear. Until then, he'd do well to remember that it was wise to mark his words carefully.

"Red Cheeks!" Wawaneechotinka abruptly cried, making no pretense at being quiet.

Davy had heard it too. The thud of heavy paws hammering the earth. A snarl ripped the dark, a snarl that reverberated as if it issued from the depths of a bottomless well. He sped off, bracing her as best he was able, plowing through brush, trampling high grass and weeds, the grizzly growing closer and closer, so close now that its breathing reminded him of the wheeze of a blacksmith's bellows, so close that in another few seconds it would be on them.

Then the vegetation parted and before them glistened the surface of a wide waterway. Without hesitation Davy plunged in, the water so cold that it jolted his already primed senses. It came as high as his waist, rising rapidly as he surged further out. To his chest it climbed. To his neck.

Wawaneechotinka clung to him as if for dear life. Her whole body became diamond hard, and Davy did not need to look back to know why. But he did anyway, and froze.

On the bank loomed a hulking mountain of sinew, rapier teeth, and sword-like claws. The grizzly had stopped at the water's edge. It was sniffing loudly.

Davy stood firm, resisting the tug of the current. He prayed they were invisible against the backdrop of darkly flowing water. The stream would mask their scent, so unless they made a sound, the bear might have no notion of where they were.

Growling ferociously, the silver-tip padded from side to side, its head bobbing and swaying.

The maiden trembled. Davy held her tighter to calm her, but she shook like a falling leaf. Afraid she would give them away, he pressed her head down on his shoulder. Her lips closed on his neck, lingering in a spontaneous grateful kiss.

A roar blasted from the bank, a roar so loud it raised the short hairs on the nape of Davy's neck, a roar so bestial it made him want to resume running.

The grizzly could not find them and was growing madder by the moment. It paced. It snarled. It grumbled to itself just as a cranky man would do. For an eternity it did all this. Finally, it turned to take its leave.

Wawaneechotinka exhaled in relief.

Like a striking rattler the immense creature pivoted and took two long strides into the stream. Head uplifted, it sniffed and sniffed.

Davy's heart missed a beat. Or so it felt as he dipped lower, the water rising as high as his chin. The grizzly was no more than ten feet away, its massive head starkly silhouetted against the stars. He swore that he could see its nostrils widening.

The Ojibwa maiden faced her moment of truth. Her body shook so hard that Davy nearly lost his grip. Her breathing was erratic. He recognized the signs. In another few seconds either her fear would overwhelm her and provoke her into doing something they would both regret, or she would marshal her self-control.

It was the latter. After a last convulsive shudder,

Wawaneechotinka reined in her tumultuous emotions. Relaxing in his grasp, she stared boldly at the grizzly as if inwardly defying it to charge them.

From one extreme to the other, Davy mused, not taking his own eyes off the hairy colossus. It was moving slowly upstream, parallel to the bank. The bear acted as if it had caught their scent, but whatever it was smelling was plainly not them. Davy had to clamp a lid on an urge to whoop for joy when the grizzly splashed on around a bend.

For the longest while neither Davy nor Wawaneechotinka moved. Davy strained his ears until his head hurt, but he did not hear any evidence that the bear was in their vicinity. He glanced at the maiden, who nodded, then helped her to the opposite bank. It was steeper than the other. Both of them were so soaked, their moccasins so slippery, that they had to climb to the top on their hands and knees.

Exhausted, Wawaneechotinka lay on her belly and rested her head on her arms. "I sleep for one moon," she said wearily.

"Not yet you don't," Davy cautioned. He wouldn't put it past the grizzly to return. Forking his hands under her shoulders, he heaved her upright. Quite by accident his hands slipped on her slick dress, his palms sliding up onto her breasts. She gasped. So did he, instantly jerking his hands off as if they had been scorched.

"Sorry," Davy blurted. So ingrained was his respect for womanhood that he figured she would be outraged and wallop him so hard his teeth would come loose. Instead, that perplexing grin of hers spread across her lovely features.

76

Homecoming

"You say one thing, do another. Maybe you not want go home. Maybe you really want stay."

Wonderful! Davy thought. Choosing not to comment, he pushed on through the undergrowth until he struck a small clearing. Since in another hour or so it would be daylight, he saw no sense in pressing on. "We'll rest here," he suggested.

"We must dry clothes," Wawaneechotinka said, and just like that she bent to peel off her dress.

"Hold on!" Davy declared, spinning so he would not see something he was not meant to. Her brazen behavior shocked him, until he recalled that among some tribes nakedness was not viewed as shameful. There had been one in North Carolina where the women walked around as boldly as could be with not so much as a stitch of clothing from their waists up.

He'd heard no reports one way or the other about the Chippewas. So he could not say whether Wawaneechotinka was doing what came naturally to her, or whether it was a ruse to entice him into changing his mind about going back to Tennessee.

"I need to dry mine too," Davy said, "but we both should have some privacy." He walked toward a thicket. "I'll go behind here so you can spread your dress out as you like. Give a yell if you need me."

Wawaneechotinka was disappointed. "There be enough room for both," she said. "I not mind."

"I would," Davy said. She must have thought he was being ridiculous. So would quite a few fellow backwoodsmen he could name. But he couldn't help it. His ma had drilled into his head the ideal that all women were to be treated like ladies, whether they were ladies or not. White or red or black, it was of no consequence.

Once the thicket sheltered him, Davy sat and took off his powder horn, ammo pouch, and leather bag. The lead balls in the ammo pouch were wet, but all he had to do was spread them out for the air to dry. No water had gotten into the powder horn, so his black powder was fine. A few of his personal effects he wiped off with handfuls of grass.

Both pistols and the rifle had to be dried, cleaned, and reloaded. He draped his shirt and leggings over low limbs, but left his underthings on in case Wawaneechotinka paid him a visit.

Everything tended to, Davy plopped onto his back. He drifted asleep as the first pale streaks of pink in the eastern sky heralded the advent of another dawn. When next he opened his eyes, he was mildly surprised to discover the sun was straight overhead. He had slept half the day away.

The lead balls and the rest were dry. His clothes and coonskin cap were slightly damp, but he put them on anyway. Circling the thicket, he stopped short of the clearing and called out softly, "Rise and shine, woman. Time's a-wasting. We have to be on our way."

When Wawaneechotinka did not answer, Davy said it again. Troubled by her failure to acknowledge him a second time, he dared to take a peek.

The clearing was empty.

Davy strode into the open. "Wawaneechotinka?" he yelled, but not too loudly in case the grizzly was within earshot. She failed to answer. Worried, he crossed the clearing, passed through the brush, and came out on the bank of the stream.

Homecoming

The tinkle of laughter came from a shallow pool to the right. Davy turned toward it—and wished he hadn't. For frolicking naked in the middle was the Chippewa maiden. She laughed again as a flush crept up his face and he put his back to her. "You should have warned me," he scolded.

"Why you act so?" Wawaneechotinka asked. "You say you have two wives. You must see women without clothes."

"I wish," Davy said to himself. To her, he declared, "My wives have been the kind who only bare themselves when the lights are out. I never saw my first or my second without their clothes on in broad daylight."

Wawaneechotinka's jaw dropped. "You joke, Red Cheeks."

"Many white women are that way," Davy revealed. "It has to do with their upbringing. White folks don't think it proper for a woman to show too much skin."

The maiden rose to her full height, water dripping from her sleek shoulders, from her shapely thighs, and from her other ample endowments. "What you think?"

"I think I'd better go for a stroll to cool down my boilers while you finish up," Davy said. Doffing his coonskin cap, he scampered westward until the pool was out of sight.

Davy let out a long breath. He mopped his brow and filled his head with favorite images of his wife. "Elizabeth, Elizabeth," he said. "If only you knew how hard I try to be true, maybe you wouldn't be so upset when I go off on a gallivant."

From his possibles bag Davy took a piece of jerked venison packed for him weeks ago by Elizabeth. The tangy scent reminded him of the delicious aroma that had filled their cabin when she prepared it. The smooth texture reminded him of the feel of her, of the embrace they had shared shortly before he left. A wave of longing washed over him. He missed her keenly, more than he had at any other point during the trek.

"A sure enough sign I should head home," Davy told himself. Which he would, just as soon as he escorted Wawaneechotinka to her people and rounded up Flavius.

That reminded him. Where could his friend be? Knowing Harris, he was probably holed up somewhere waiting for Davy to find him, all the while gorging himself on rabbit stew or whatever else he bagged.

Flavius had a knack for making the best of the worst situations.

At that very moment, miles to the northwest, Flavius Harris glumly picked at a flea crawling up his leg. Crushing the insect, he threw it aside. The motion of his arm attracted one of the village mongrels, which came close and growled, baring its vicious teeth.

"Go pester someone else," Flavius said, kicking dirt at it. A score of times during the day a dog had approached to sniff and snarl, but as yet none had seen fit to take a bite out of him.

The word "bite" brought to mind the subject of food. His stomach imitated a riled chipmunk, reminding him that he had not eaten since the evening before when the old woman had brought him the mash. He'd give anything for another bite of her concoction.

As if she had read his thoughts, the Ojibwa woman came out of her wigwam bearing a birch-bark bowl.

Leaning heavily on her cane, she walked with an uneven gait to the post.

Flavius smiled, receiving a scowl in response. His mouth watering at the prospect of eating, he inhaled the tantalizing odor. He eagerly reached out, then yelped.

The old woman had rapped him on the knuckles. She spoke sternly, wagging her cane, as if she were scolding an errant child. Bobbing her bony chin at the bowl, she said, "Manomini."

"Thank you," Flavius said, taking that as a sign that he could help himself. For his audacity he was rapped once more. She could flick that cane of hers faster than a bee could flick its stinger, and the cane hurt a lot more.

"What's the matter with you?" Flavius groused, rubbing his hand. "Quit playing with me. If I'm entitled to eat, give me the food and go away."

The woman tapped the bowl. "Manomini," she repeated.

Flavius had an inspiration. "Manomini," he said, not having the slightest idea what it meant. His hunch proved accurate. Grinning, she offered the mash, and did not hit him when he gingerly accepted it.

As the woman limped away, Flavius dipped his fingers and shoveled some into his mouth. He had learned his lesson the day before. Rather than wolf it down in ten seconds flat, he ate slowly, a tiny bit at a time, drawing the meal out so that it took him fifteen minutes to clean the bowl.

He longed for seconds. In vain he watched the old woman's wigwam with the aim of getting her attention should she reappear. An hour elapsed. Then two.

His stomach rumbled the entire time.

At the rate he was going, Flavius mused, he'd be skin and bones before the three days were up.

Around a wigwam came Keekweechiweepinank and Kawakatusk, in earnest conversation. They slanted toward him, the leader's visage etched in displeasure.

Flavius set the bowl down and rose onto his knees. "Howdy," he greeted them. "Any sign of my friend yet?"

The Ojibwa leader had his hands clasped behind his back. His brow puckered as he fixed the Tennessean with an icy glare. "Many warriors out looking. Some find tracks." Keekweechiweepinank paused. "Your friend take sister on his horse."

"I could have told you that," Flavius said. "It was the only way he could save her from those other Indians."

"Is so? Then why they not ride this way?" the chief demanded. "They be here by now."

Flavius did not know, so he shrugged.

Keekweechiweepinank gestured at the blazing orb that dominated the sky, well on its downward arc. "Soon sun set. That leave you two sleeps."

"Davy will be here," Flavius insisted, but he did not sound confident, even to himself. His anxiety was transparent. The old warrior stepped nearer, rattling words, and patted him on the shoulder.

"Kawakatusk say not to be afraid," Keekweechiweepinank translated. "If friend not come, Kawakatusk will kill you fast so you not suffer."

"He's all heart."

Chapter Seven

Davy Crockett sorely missed his mount. Whereas on horseback they could travel at the rate of four or five miles an hour, on foot they crawled along at a snail's pace. Due to the rough terrain, they covered only seven miles or so by twilight.

According to what Wawaneechotinka told him, it would take five days to reach her village. Possibly more. That was much too long to suit him. Who knows what trouble Flavius could get into in that time?

Davy shuddered to think how long it would be before he saw Tennessee again. Unless he acquired another horse, he'd be a candidate for a rocking chair by the time he got there. Unfortunately, in that neck of the woods, horses were as scarce as hen's teeth.

"What you thinking, Red Cheeks?" the maiden inquired as they crested a rise. Below was a narrow valley divided by two streams.

"Nothing much," Davy fibbed. To tell the truth invited her to point out that he need not return home at all, and he'd had quite enough of that, thank you. "Let's locate a spot to make camp. Looks as if we get to spend another night together."

A gleam came into Wawaneechotinka's eyes. "I be glad," she said.

Davy wanted to kick a stump. He didn't know which was worse, matching wits with Kiyo Kaga or with her. In a way he should be flattered that Wawaneechotinka had set her sights on him, but it created all sorts of complications he would rather not deal with.

He recollected his grandpa saying once that when a woman threw her noose over a man, there wasn't much the man could do except stand there and let her tighten it or run like hell. Davy would have lit out long since if not for the fix she was in.

Soon they came to a clearing beside a stream. There wasn't a cloud in the sky, but that didn't stop Davy from studying the heavens and announcing, "We might get some heavy rain before dawn. I'd best see to it that you'll be comfortable."

"Rain?" Wawaneechotinka said quizzically, scanning the firmament. "I see no sign."

"Trust me," Davy said as innocently as could be. "Tennesseeans are famous throughout the country for being able to read the weather better than anyone else. Why, there was a widow lady once over to Greene County who was so good at predicting the weather, she could do it for a whole year in advance. Folks would come to her from miles around. One farmer paid her a visit every January regular as clockwork to learn what the weather was going to be like during planting season in late April and May."

As Davy talked, he busied himself gathering long limbs from under a nearby tree. He had quite a pile before Wawaneechotinka took notice.

"You plan make big fire?"

"This is for the lean-to," Davy revealed. "You're going to be as warm and snug as an old bedbug tonight."

"That be nice," Wawaneechotinka said, her sly grin reappearing.

It was all Davy could do not to bust a gut. She figured that she had him right where she wanted him, but she was about to learn that he could be as clever as a fox when he had to be. Whistling softly, he erected the lean-to in record time, and stood back to admire his handwork. It wasn't much to boast of, lacking sides as it did, and with the branches that formed the shelter spaced too far apart to keep out any rain.

"Here you go," Davy declared, escorting her by the elbow inside. She stooped and sat, then patted the ground beside her.

"There not much room. You and I must sleep close." Wawaneechotinka pressed her hands together to show exactly how close.

"Wouldn't think of it," Davy said, moving around to the other side of the fire. "A true gentleman would never intrude on a lady's privacy. I'm sleeping out here where I can keep my eyes peeled for the Fox war party."

Wawaneechotinka's fine spirits were gone with the wind. "If you not sleep inside, I not too."

Davy adopted a hurt expression. "After all the trouble I went to on your behalf? That would be terribly rude. Most white folks would take it as a sign that you didn't like them."

"I like you," Wawaneechotinka declared without thinking.

Davy had her dead to rights. Casually reclining on his left side, he commented, "Then I know you'll do what's proper and sleep in there like you should."

It was a long night. Wawaneechotinka sulked for hours. Davy could tell that she was picking her brain for a way to beat him at his own game. When along about midnight he suggested that they turn in, she gave him a look that would have withered a petrified tree.

Having been married twice and having three sisters to boot, Davy was well aware that womenfolk sometimes did not accept defeat as graciously as they ought to. So he was not the least bit surprised when Wawaneechotinka spent half the night tossing and turning and sighing and every so often slapping the earth.

Daybreak found them up and on their way, the maiden still sulking. Davy paused frequently to check their back trail, but saw no hint of pursuit.

The sun was directly overhead when they rested at a ribbon of a creek, the water so clear and pure that drinking it was like quaffing the nectar of the gods. Davy was on his belly, gulping the crystal cool liquid, when the heavy stomp of something big approaching rapidly from the rear brought him to his feet in a rush.

With Wawaneechotinka at his side, Davy darted into undergrowth that bordered the game trail they had been following. He guessed that an elk was as thirsty as they were. A low nicker proved him wrong.

Davy's sorrel pranced into the clearing and looked

around. Its sides were flecked with sweat and grime. Its legs bore scores of nicks and abrasions. Burrs were tangled in its mane and tail, brush tangled in the reins. Yet that animal was the finest horse Davy had ever beheld. Forgetting himself, he burst from concealment and nearly spooked it into running off.

"Hold on, fella!" Davy said, getting a grip on the bridle. "It's me." He stroked its neck, scratched behind its ears, and nearly had the sorrel calmed down when Wawaneechotinka stepped into the open. One whiff of her scent and the horse shied and tried to bolt again. Davy clung on, talking softly while rubbing it, and in due course the sorrel was as tame as ever.

"How he find us, Red Cheeks?" Wawaneechotinka asked in a rare moment of near-flawless English.

"He's part bloodhound, I reckon," Davy said proudly. He'd heard stories about dogs and cats that traveled great distances to find their owners, but he'd never heard tell of a horse tracking its master down as this one had done. When they got back to Tennessee, he was going to treat it to a week of rest and all the sweet hay it could eat.

"Now we can make good time," Davy said. But he was the only one happy at the news.

The sorrel deserved a rubdown. Davy stripped off the saddle, which had come partly loose. Large blisters covered one shoulder where the leather had chafed the hide. He lanced each blister and applied a cool mud pack.

Wawaneechotinka acted as skittish around the horse as it was around her. She hesitantly touched it a few times, and once was bold enough to rub its neck.

"So big. So strong. Why horses let people ride them?"

"For the same reason dogs and cats take a shine to folks," Davy said as he pried a burr from the sorrel's mane. "Some critters just naturally get along with us. Some don't."

"Is right, you think?"

No one had ever asked that question of Davy before, and he cocked an eyebrow at her, not quite sure of her meaning. "Right how? Do you mean is it right for us to keep dogs as pets and have horses tote us all over creation?"

"Yes."

At that moment the sorrel affectionately nuzzled him, nearly dumping him off his feet. Chuckling, Davy responded, "There's your answer. If cats didn't want to roost in our laps and purr themselves silly, they'd fight shy of us. If dogs didn't like our company, they'd all live off in packs in the wild. And if horses didn't like to be rode, they'd buck us off and stomp us to death." He paused to tickle the sorrel's chin. "Some do, mind you. But by and large I think the Good Lord meant for us and them to get along, or He wouldn't've put us all on the same planet."

Wawaneechotinka gazed across the pristine valley. "White men dig in earth to plant seeds. I have seen them."

More puzzled than ever, Davy said, "Farming, we call that. What about it?"

"Is wrong. People must not wound our Mother."

At last Davy saw where her trail was leading. Some tribes regarded the Earth as their literal and supreme

Homecoming

Mother and worshipped her much as his kind did the Creator.

"Man in dress want us to plant seeds," Wawaneechotinka went on. "Him say we never go hungry again. Him say we plant many things, eat many things." She gestured at the wilderness. "But we not go hungry. We have what he call wild rice and onions and more. We have berries. We have fish and deer and moose. Our Mother give us all food we need."

Davy was not about to argue with sentiments like those. He knew firsthand the marvels of nature's bounty. An experienced backwoodsman, he never needed to go into town for a single thing if he did not want to. The woods supplied all he needed. In that respect the Ojibwas and he were a lot alike.

"My brother be angry with man in dress," Wawaneechotinka explained. "So him go off to teach Winnebagos, and they kill him."

The priest should have left well enough alone, Davy mused. Some Indians didn't take to having the white man's beliefs shoved down their throats, even on so simple a matter as tilling the soil.

The sorrel had been rubbed from head to hooves, so Davy threw on the blanket and saddle and mounted. Wawaneechotinka had to be coaxed up, then glued her full form to his.

"I like this, Red Cheeks."

"Figured you would."

"Long way to village," she mentioned, quite pleased that it was the case. Her breath prickled his neck. "Who know what maybe happen?"

Davy Crockett applied his heels, wishing that his horse was gifted with the speed of a shooting star.

89

Come to think of it, even that wouldn't be fast enough if Wawaneechotinka took it into her head to employ her feminine charms to their full effect.

It reminded Davy of something his pa once said. "Mark my words, son. There are three natural forces against which men are downright helpless: hurricanes, tornadoes, and willful women."

"What's a body to do?" Davy had asked.

"With the first two, just hunker down and wait them out. Sooner or later hurricanes end and tornadoes go elsewhere."

"What about willful women? There must be something we can do there."

Until he started courting, Davy never had understood why his pa threw back his head and laughed.

Flavius Harris was idly doodling in the dirt with a stick when a ruckus broke out at the south end of the village. He jumped to his feet, praying it was Davy and the pretty filly. A wigwam blocked his view, so it was a while before he saw three warriors, at the head of a large crowd, guiding his dun.

It startled Flavius. He didn't see how the men had gotten the horse to the island without it getting wet, yet it was as dry as tinder. There had to be a secret trail, he realized, a link to the mainland that would be worth his while to discover.

Keekweechiweepinank stepped from a dwelling and met the trio. After a lengthy palaver, the Ojibwa leader and those assembled came toward the post.

Involuntarily, Flavius backed up until he bumped against it. Quelling an uneasy feeling, he cleared his throat. "Something I can do for you?"

Homecoming

The chief had a red blanket over his shoulders. Sweeping it aside, he indicated the dun. "This animal be yours, white man?"

"That it is," Flavius admitted. "What of it?"

The hapless dun was much the worse for wear. Mud caked it clear up to the brisket. Its tail was so tangled that it would take a week of Sundays to brush it straight again. A deep gash on the right foreleg below the elbow was coated with dried blood. On its flank were long scratch marks.

Claw marks, Flavius judged them, either from a lynx or a bobcat. Out of concern, he advanced to inspect the wounds, and was rudely shoved by one of the warriors.

Flavius came close to throwing himself at the culprit. "There was no call for that, you cussed heathen!" he fumed. "I only want to take care of my horse, is all. Can't you see that it's been hurt?"

"You care for this animal?" Keekweechiweepinank asked in a tone that implied he found the likelihood hard to believe.

"What a stupid question!" Flavius snapped. He knew he might be digging his own grave, but he no longer gave a damn. He was sick and tired of being treated as if he were pond scum, of being pushed and prodded and looked down on just because the color of his skin happened to be different from theirs. He barreled past the warrior who had shoved him, and gently ran a hand over the dun's scratches. They were not particularly deep. Whatever had attacked the horse had either been too small or too slow to get a firm grip. None of the slashes, thankfully, was infected. He reached for the cinch, and was lightly jabbed in the back by a lance tip.

"What you do?" Keekweechiweepinank asked. "Maybe try to escape?"

Flavius tapped the saddle. "Ever worn a pair of tight moccasins too long? This has been on him since your men captured me. It should come off." Heedless of the risk, he swatted the lance aside and hastily undid the cinch. A warrior took the saddle from him as he lowered it. The same with the saddle blanket.

"We keep them for you," Keekweechiweepinank stated.

"You hold all the cards," Flavius replied, boiling with resentment. He checked the dun's back and all four legs. It was weary and sore and no doubt hungry, but it was better off than he was. One more day and he'd be crow bait.

The Ojibwas observed everything he did with great interest. Kawakatusk had arrived, and huddled with Keekweechiweepinank. When they turned, the leader stepped up to the dun and rather timidly patted its neck.

"I want you teach me ride, white man."

Flavius could have been floored with a feather. "Why should I?" he countered. "You're fixing to make wolf meat of me in another sleep, or have you forgotten? Teach yourself, Mr. High-and-Mighty."

Keekweechiweepinank, surprisingly, was not offended. "I let you live as long as it take. Is that good?"

Flavius was all set to call the chief every nasty name he could think of when a keg of black powder went off inside his head. Here was the answer to his prayers! The Ojibwas would have to untie him in order for him to do the job right, and once free he could make his bid to escape. Forcing himself to stay calm in order not to arouse their suspicions, he asked, "Why this sudden interest in learning to ride?"

Keekweechiweepinank was gaining confidence with every stroke. He placed a hand on the dun's muzzle, then slid it onto its nose. The horse snorted and nipped at his fingers, missing by a fraction.

Afraid that the chief would change his mind if the dun kicked up a fuss, Flavius said, "Don't take that personal. Some horses don't like to be touched around the mouth, even those used to a bit."

The Ojibwa leader was examining his hand. "My interest not sudden," he answered. "When I was boy, white men come to our village. Trappers on horses. Ever since, I want to ride as they did. I want to understand why your kind like it so much."

Flavius snickered. "What's to understand? Riding horses sure beats riding porcupines." Soothing the dun, he commented, "This animal is tuckered out. That's why it is so irritable. Let me clean it up and feed it, and come morning I'll give you your first lesson."

Keekweechiweepinank glanced at him.

"Keep me under guard the whole time if you don't trust me," Flavius said, knowing full well the man didn't. "After I'm done, I'll show your warriors how to hobble it so it won't run off on you in the middle of the night." The real reason, of course, was that he did not want the dun running off on *him* before he effected his escape.

"We do as you say," Keekweechiweepinank said, and relayed instructions to the three warriors who had brought the dun to the village.

The crowd dispersed. Flavius was thrilled to the bone when one of the men untied his ankle. The trio hovered over him like bees over a flower, ringing him at all times. But they did not interfere when he took the dun to the lake to wash off the mud and treat the scratch marks. Nor did they object when he walked the horse to a tract of grass so it could graze.

Flavius had a hunch that there was more to the chief's request than Keekweechiweepinank let on. He was not going to pry, though, and risk antagonizing Keekweechiweepinank when he was so close to ending the nightmare.

True to his word, Flavius demonstrated how a horse should be hobbled. His guards then returned him to the post and secured the rope to his leg.

That night, it was next to impossible to sleep. Flavius pondered until the wee hours, plotting ways of making his break. All involved an element of risk. Yes, he might take an arrow in the back for his effort, but he would rather go down fighting than be butchered like a hog at Easter.

Flavius did not realize he had dozed until the cry of an infant brought him around shortly before the sun rose. He was so nervous that his legs shook as if he had the ague. So much was literally riding on what would happen that he was as tightly strung as a fiddle.

The old lady with the cane brought him a bowl of mash for breakfast, which was unusual. Normally she fed him in the evening. This time she'd also added strips of meat, which he slipped into his pocket. They would come in handy later when he was on his own in the wilds.

It galled Flavius that Keekweechiweepinank did not

show up until the middle of the morning. By then his nerves were frayed to the breaking point, so much so that when the leader came up behind him and spoke, Flavius nearly jumped out of his skin.

"I am ready if you are."

Flavius composed himself, saying, "I was beginning to think you had changed your mind." Attending the chief were the same three warriors from the day before as well as several dozen curious Ojibwas, among them Kawakatusk and Tokawonda. Flavius had to hide his annoyance. The more who were there, the more difficult it would be for him to get clean away.

Keekweechiweepinank himself untied the rope. Flavius made a show of rubbing his leg to restore circulation. Secretly, he scoured the perimeter of the village for the trail that had to be there. Yet as near as he could tell, at no point was there a connecting link between the island and the mainland.

"We begin," Keekweechiweepinank announced, grandly leading the way.

Flavius was hemmed in by the three warriors. He put on a friendly air to lull the Ojibwas into thinking that he was as harmless as a newborn kitten. Smiling at the children and nodding at the men and women, he was brought to the dun.

The chief extended an arm. Flavius held his breath, dreading that the horse would chomp off a finger or two and spoil everything. For once the contrary critter behaved, and merely flinched when Keekweechiweepinank petted it. The Ojibwas were mightily impressed by their leader's audacity, more so when he looped an arm around the dun's neck as if they were the best of pards.

The horse stamped a hoof, a definite sign that it did not like being so close to a complete stranger. Flavius quickly went up and bent to remove the hobbles, declaring, "First things first. Have your men fetch the saddle and blanket and I'll throw them on."

The request was relayed. Keekweechiweepinank studied every step of the saddling. Flavius let him tighten the cinch and loosen it a few times to get the feel of how it was done. Then came the moment of truth, the glorious moment Flavius had waited all night for, the moment when he stepped into the stirrups and forked leather. He did so slowly so as not to cause alarm.

"See? Wasn't that easy?" Flavius asked Keekweechiweepinank. "Now comes the tricky part, actually riding. The key is in the reins." To demonstrate, Flavius flicked them and walked the dun in a wide circle. The onlookers moved back to give him room, just as he wanted them to. He exaggerated reining up, explaining, "This is how you stop."

Keekweechiweepinank motioned. "My turn," he said eagerly.

"Not quite yet," Flavius said. "There's one more basic thing you need to learn." He straightened. The shoreline was thirty feet away. Another forty feet beyond was the bank of a stream that fed into the small lake. All he had to do was reach it and he would be safe.

Flavius gulped. He was scared. But as Davy liked to say, he had it to do. With a whip of the reins and a flap of his legs, he made his move.

GET YOUR 4 FREE BOOKS NOW— A VALUE BETWEEN $16 AND $20

Mail the Free Book Certificate Today!

FREE BOOKS CERTIFICATE!

YES! I want to subscribe to the Leisure Western Book Club. Please send my 4 FREE BOOKS. Then, each month, I'll receive the four newest Leisure Western Selections to preview FREE for 10 days. If I decide to keep them, I will pay the Special Members Only discounted price of just $3.36 each, a total of $13.44. This saves me between $3 and $6 off the bookstore price. There are no shipping, handling or other charges. There is no minimum number of books I must buy and I may cancel the program at any time. In any case, the 4 FREE BOOKS are mine to keep—at a value of between $17 and $20! Offer valid only in the USA.

Name_____

Address_____

City_____ State_____

Zip_____ Phone_____

Biggest Savings Offer!

For those of you who would like to pay us in advance by check or credit card—we've got an even bigger savings in mind. Interested? Check here. ☐

If under 18, parent or guardian must sign.
Terms, prices and conditions subject to change. Subscription subject to acceptance. Leisure Books reserves the right to reject any order or cancel any subscription.

GET FOUR BOOKS TOTALLY *FREE*—A VALUE BETWEEN $16 AND $20

**PLEASE RUSH
MY FOUR FREE
BOOKS TO ME
RIGHT AWAY!**

Leisure Western Book Club
P.O. Box 6613
Edison, NJ 08818-6613

AFFIX
STAMP
HERE

Chapter Eight

Thirty feet can seem like a mile when a man is flanked by hostile Indians who would as soon see him dead as look at him.

Flavius Harris counted on the Ojibwas being so taken aback by his break for freedom that they would not let an arrow fly or hurl a lance before he reached the water. In this respect he was woefully mistaken, for no sooner had the dun loped forward than a shaft buzzed past his ear like an enraged wasp. Shouts broke out. Feet pounded. A lance nearly added a part to his hair.

Bent low, Flavius flailed the reins. He knew that the dun was as fond of water as he was, but he hoped that in this instance the horse would have the common sense not to balk and would plunge right in. He should have known better.

They were ten feet from the lake when the dun suddenly dug in its hooves and locked its legs, its rump dipping so close to the ground that Flavius was almost dumped from the saddle. He hauled on the reins with all his strength, but the horse kept on sliding, swept by its momentum into the water. The dun flung itself to the right, twisting to scramble onto dry land.

In desperation Flavius flung himself toward the far bank. He would rather drown than be tortured to death. Churning his limbs like a windmill gone berserk, for the first time in his life he endeavored to swim. To his amazement, he succeeded! But not for long. After traveling all of six feet, he inexplicably lost speed, then began to sink.

Panic numbed him. He neglected to churn, and immediately sank like a rock. Inadvertently, Flavius opened his mouth to scream. Water poured in instead. He gasped. He blubbered. He strove furiously to regain the surface. The murky, cold water dragged on his clothes, pulling him lower.

The end was near. Flavius stopped struggling. He had done his best and it had not been good enough. His only regret was that he would never see Matilda again.

An image of her rotund features floated before him. Flavius reached out for it under the impression that he could touch her. His fingers brushed a solid object.

Vaguely, Flavius felt hands wrap around his arms, hands fork under his shoulders, hands grip him by the back of his buckskin shirt. He was wrenched up out of the water and flung landward. His legs wobbled, and he would have toppled had another Ojibwa not seized him and thrust him into the shallows.

Sucking in precious air, Flavius blinked to clear his

vision. His legs buckled. He fell to his knees in inches-deep water and wiped a hand across his face.

Half a dozen warriors were in the lake with him. Two others had retrieved the dun. Jamming the shore were scores of Ojibwas, their countenances like those Flavius had once seen at a funeral. At the forefront was Keekweechiweepinank, and he was the most somber of the bunch.

"You try trick me, white man."

What could Flavius say? There was no denying the truth. He placed his hands flat to rise, but a pair of brawny warriors beat him to it. Jerked erect, he was forced up the incline and made to kneel in front of the chief.

"I maybe let you live you done what I want," the leader said.

"How was I to know?" Flavius rasped.

Keekweechiweepinank frowned. "You bring this on self." Removing the red blanket, he handed it to a warrior, who gave him a war club in exchange. Keekweechiweepinank gripped the handle and hefted the deadly weapon several times. "Your end be quick. There be no pain."

Flavius had recovered enough to spit out, "Don't do me any favors, damn you! You're nothing but a red butcher!" It had been a petty outburst, but Flavius could not help himself. He was about to die.

The war club slowly rose. Flavius stared at the rounded head complete with vicious studs. The chief had powerful shoulders. One blow was all it would take. He braced himself, silently mouthing the Lord's Prayer.

Keekweechiweepinank tensed for the killing stroke.

David Thompson

"*Stop!* Hold it right there!"

The outcry came from the east side of the village. Flavius, like everyone else, glanced around. Unlike everyone else, his eyes filled with tears.

Davy Crockett held his long rifle at his side as he approached the Ojibwas astride his sorrel. He did not draw a pistol or unlimber his tomahawk. He wanted to do nothing they would construe as a threat. Plastering a smile on his face, he said good-naturedly to the man with the war club, "My friend's noggin is as hard as iron. You're liable to break that overgrown stick of yours if you hit him."

Keekweechiweepinank appeared as astounded as the rest of his people. Slowly lowering his weapon, he demanded, "Who are you? How you get here?"

"Folks call me Davy," Crockett said. "As for how I found your charming village, you can thank this lovely lady for showing me the trail." Shifting, he nodded at Wawaneechotinka, who had grown strangely quiet the past few miles. He did not add that she had not been in any rush to get home. That she had, in fact, done her best to delay them by having him make frequent stops and dragging her heels when it was time to saddle up.

Davy winked at Flavius, whose mouth hung open wide enough to snag a blackbird on the wing. Greeting everyone he passed by saying, "Howdy!" or "How do!" he drew rein near the tall warrior who had been about to slay his friend. "Hope you don't mind me dropping in like this," he said as he dismounted, "but I had to fetch Wawaneechotinka back. A Fox warrior by the name of Kiyo Kaga tried to steal her."

At the mention of the dreaded Fox leader, murmuring spread among the Ojibwas.

"You took long time bring her," Keekweechiweepinank said, his mistrust as thick as jam on bread.

Davy went on smiling anyway. "It's not my fault," he retorted amiably. "Those polecats captured us. Took me a while to slip loose, then we had to run for our lives. If my horse hadn't shown up on its own we would still be wandering around out there with the Fox war party dogging our heels." He helped Wawaneechotinka down. "You must know this lady. She's one of your own. And now she's back safe and sound."

The tall warrior tossed the club to another. "Wawaneechotinka is my sister. I am Keekweechiweepinank, leader of my people."

Davy figured that brother and sister would leap into each other's arms, but they merely stood and stared fondly at one another. Some tribal customs were like that. Public displays of affection between members of the opposite sex, even blood kin, were frowned upon.

The old woman who had been with Wawaneechotinka at the hill came rushing up. Uttering a high-pitched yip, she hugged the maiden, who reciprocated.

Her mother, Davy recollected as he sidled over to Flavius, who had yet to close his mouth. Clapping his friend on the back, he said in Flavius's ear, "On your feet. We have to get out of here while they're preoccupied." Aloud, he declared. "Well, let's get going. I'm sure the chief will do what is right and let us go our way now that I've brought his sister home."

Keekweechiweepinank turned. "You be tired and hungry. After what you do for us, we must show gratitude. You not leave just yet."

Davy steered Flavius toward the dun. "No need to put yourselves out on our account," he said cheerily. "We'll rustle up some food on our own." Waving merrily at the Ojibwas, he called out, "It's been a pleasure meeting you folks. If you're ever down in the Obion Lake country of west Tennessee, be sure and look us up."

At a command from Keekweechiweepinank, four warriors positioned themselves in front of the horses. The chief locked his gaze on Davy's. "I insist you stay."

"If you put it that way," Davy said as the Indians pressed in closer.

They were called the Midewiwin, or Grand Medicine Society. They were the spiritual standard-bearers of the Ojibwas, and they had organized a special ceremony to commemorate the safe deliverance of Wawaneechotinka and Tokawonda.

The Medicine Dance, it was called. Keekweechiweepinank told Davy that no other white men had ever been privileged to attend one.

"We're flattered," Davy said, and meant it. The tribe was bestowing a great honor on Flavius and him, akin to the President of the United States holding a formal ball for a visiting foreign dignitary. He nudged his friend. "Aren't we flattered, hoss?"

Flavius nodded. He was trying, but he could not marshal much enthusiasm when he really wanted to be as far from the Ojibwa village as possible. He wouldn't put it past Keekweechiweepinank to act friendly just so they would lower their guard and be easy to wipe out later.

Pounding drums echoed across the small lake. The

entire tribe was gathered around a unique lodge. It had no outer covering, consisting solely of a framework of slender saplings that formed a wide tunnel. Gaily dressed members of the Midewiwin Society entered in single file at one end and emerged from the other, dancing in time to the beat of the drums and a chorus of singers.

Davy had long been fascinated by Indian ceremonies. It never ceased to amaze him that seldom did two tribes share the same ones. In Tennessee there were tribes that lived no more than a hundred miles apart and had virtually nothing in common. Their religious beliefs, how their leaders were selected, their clothes, their weapons, everything was as different as night from day.

It had been the same in Florida and elsewhere.

Davy had long harbored the belief that if the various tribes had been better organized when the first white men sailed to North America, history would have taken a different course.

For more generations than the members of most tribes could remember, they had been at war with one or more other tribes. The constant bloodletting had left them disorganized to such an extent that it had been relatively simple for the influx of white settlers to exterminate those tribes that resisted or else push them deeper into the wilderness.

There was even talk of rounding up every last Indian east of the Mississippi and driving them west. Serious talk. In the highest councils of the government the issue was being debated.

Most of Davy's kin and neighbors were in favor of the idea. They saw it as an easy fix to a problem that had been plaguing whites since Jamestown. They wanted the Army to do the rounding up to give the forced exodus official sanction. But they squawked at having taxpayers foot the bill.

They also squawked whenever Davy mentioned that he was against the plan. "What in tarnation is wrong with you?" they would rail. "Are you insane? Or have you turned into an Injun lover?"

Davy had every reason to hate Indians as much as anyone else. His grandparents had been massacred by them. He had fought in the Creek War. He had seen many Creek atrocities firsthand.

Yet Davy had also seen white atrocities. He had observed cruelty to Indians that downright sickened him. Neither side could claim to be totally innocent in that regard.

Then there was what Davy liked to refer to as "the incident." He had been off hunting with several men when he had taken ill. There had been no warning. He had grown feverish and weak and keeled over within minutes, unable to lift so much as a little finger.

The attack had left him completely helpless. As he lay there, limp and caked with sweat and scared out of his wits, the other hunters, his *friends*, had discussed the problem and decided that the best thing to do was to leave him!

They'd figured that he was at death's door. Besides, a couple of them had been worried that whatever had felled him might be contagious, and they had not been about to linger and risk sharing his fate.

So his *friends* had taken his rifle and effects and gone off to tell his wife and children about his demise, leaving him alone and frail and utterly defenseless—

in the heart of the wilderness.

Davy had been furious. He had wanted to curse them, to tell them that no decent human being would abandon someone in dire need, to scream that they were cowards and blackguards and worse. But all he'd been able to do was lie there and watch them walk off, helpless, listening to the crunch of their footsteps fade in the distance.

It was impossible for Davy to describe the horrible feeling that had come over him. He had lain there for hours straining his ears in the feeble hope that they would realize their mistake and come back.

The fever had worsened. Davy had felt as if he were on fire. His lungs had burned with every breath. Perspiration had cascaded off him. He had known he was fading fast. Several times he had passed out, only to awaken later feeling worse than ever.

It must have been the fourth or fifth time Davy revived that he had been startled to hear voices. *Indian* voices. Since he could not lift his head, he'd had no idea how many there were or whether they were friendly or hostile. In his fevered state he had imagined himself being scalped and mutilated, and he had prayed as he had never prayed in his life.

A hand had gently slid under his cheek and turned his face upward. Three warriors, he'd counted. The oldest, a wizened man with gray hair, had examined him much as a doctor was prone to do, even opening his eyelids wide to check his pupils.

Davy had not recognized them. They'd been from no local tribe. With him being a white man, it would have been perfectly understandable if they had gone off and left him to die, just as his friends had done.

For a few seconds Davy thought they were about to. The elderly warrior began to rise, then happened to look into his eyes. The man hesitated. His brow furrowed. Kneeling, the Indian gave directions to the other two. One toted a water skin. The older man fashioned a makeshift bowl out of bark and filled it. From a small leather pouch he took a mixture of chopped leaves and roots and added them to the water. When the concoction was thoroughly stirred, the warrior had one of his companion hold Davy's mouth open.

The taste was awful. Davy came close to gagging. It all went down, though. The Indian rose and Davy tried to thank them, but his vocal chords were as useless as the rest of him. They walked into the trees without a backward glance.

That had been the end of it, Davy reckoned. But presently the three men returned bearing a crude though serviceable litter. They carefully placed him on it, then headed eastward at a brisk clip.

Davy lost track of the number of times he lost consciousness. The journey might have been hours, it might have been days. Suddenly new voices buzzed above him. It was a woman and her two small children. The old warrior seemed to know her. A lengthy talk resulted in the warriors taking Davy into the woman's house and depositing him on a bed before they left.

The woman, a total stranger, tended him day and night for over three weeks. When she was not there, one of her children were. They fed him. They gave him water. They even bathed him and helped him use a chamber pot.

It turned out that his benefactor was a Quaker lady

who had lost her husband several years before. Most women would have called it quits and gone to live in a town where it was not quite as hard to survive. Not this one. She did the work of two, plowing fields and hunting and fishing, and at the same time doing all the work a mother normally did.

It was two weeks before Davy regained use of his voice. Two and a half before he could get out of bed and take a few steps.

Finally, when Davy was fit, the woman gave him a pouch with enough food to tide him over until he got home. On arriving, he found his family in mourning, his wife considering whether to sell their homestead, and one of his so-called *friends* already making a bid to fill Davy's moccasins.

That fall, when Davy had returned to thank the Quaker woman, her cabin was a charred ruin. The stable and the outbuildings had also been razed. Someone had burned the place to the ground. Of the widow and her children there was no sign.

Fearing the worst, Davy had galloped to the nearest settlement. Not knowing anyone there, he had gone to the parson to learn what had happened. In a horrified tone the reverend had confessed the community's dark secret, the truth piercing Davy's core like a red-hot poker.

Some of the locals had not liked the fact that the Quaker lady was on friendly terms with the Indians. Behind her back they had accused her of all manner of misdeeds, including "cavorting with redskins."

One fateful night when they were liquored up, the locals had paid her a visit. They'd gone there merely to scare her. But one thing had led to another, a drunk had set her cabin on fire, and the flames had spread to the other buildings.

The Quaker woman and her children had been trapped in their home and perished.

Davy had been in a daze when he rode out of town. Pulling off the road, he had sat on a log and cried his heart out, crying until he'd had no tears left to shed.

The boom of a drum shattered Davy Crockett's reverie. He looked up to see the dance winding down. Keekweechiweepinank, he noticed, was staring at him, and he wondered if he had committed a social blunder by allowing his attention to lapse. The chief leaned toward him.

"My sister like you."

So that was it, Davy mused. "I know."

"You not like her?"

"Whether I like or don't like doesn't matter. I have a wife back in Tennessee. I gave her my word to be true to her, and I wish I may be shot if I ever break my vow."

"You tell my sister this?"

"Of course."

Keekweechiweepinank was thoughtful a while. "So be it. Man must be true to his nature. Wawaneechotinka be upset with me, but in morning you and your friend can go. With our friendship."

Davy beamed and relayed the good news to his friend.

"Thank God!" Flavius declared. "At long last we can

head on back to our families! This ordeal is over!"

"That it is," Davy concurred.

Neither knew it then, but they were both terribly, terribly wrong.

Chapter Nine

A brilliant blue sky and a warm southerly breeze made for a spectacular day. Davy and Flavius rode out of the Ojibwa village with dogs yapping at their heels and playful children skipping alongside their horses. Every last adult had turned out for the occasion. Many smiled. A few waved, among them Keekweechiwee-pinank.

"Oh, happy day!" Flavius said. "I never thought I'd live to see this! A few more weeks and I'll be back where I belong with Matilda."

"Does this mean you don't have a hankering to do any more exploring?" Davy asked.

Flavius became agitated. "Don't tell me that you've got a notion to keep on wandering? After all we've just been through?"

Davy chuckled. "Relax. I'm as anxious to trod Tennessee soil as you are. Come hell or high water, we're bound for home, and nothing is going to stand in our way."

"Hallelujah!"

Alone among the Ojibwas, one woman was downcast. Wawaneechotinka, her arms folded across her chest, her shoulders sagging, stared sadly after the departing frontiersmen.

Flavius saw her and remarked, "That filly sure is plenty fond of you. It got her dander up when her brother said we were free to go."

"It's a crush, nothing more. She'll get over it," Davy predicted. He waved at the maiden, but she did not wave back. "She was smitten with me because I saved her from Kiyo Kaga's bunch. The same thing would have happened if it had been an Ojibwa warrior who saved her."

"Maybe so," Flavius allowed. He never had been any great shakes at figuring out females. Evidently he wasn't the only one. Matilda liked to say that when it came to women, most men were as thick as bricks. "It's best we're leaving, though. There's no telling what she would have cooked up to snare you if we'd stayed."

Davy agreed. Young women in love were apt to do foolish things. So were young men, for that matter. How well he recalled his first love, a lovely lass from North Carolina who had come to Tennessee to visit kin. In his eyes she had been the loveliest creature in existence, a ravishing vision more divine than human. Every time he'd tried to talk to her, his heart had flapped around in his chest like a chicken with its head chopped off.

His love for her had inspired him to do something he had thought he would never do: go to school. She had been a finely cultured young lady who enjoyed reading and liked to talk about the books she had enjoyed. It had been a source of excruciating embarrassment to him that he could neither read nor write, and he had resolved to remedy his ignorance right away.

Not far off had lived a man who taught school, and Davy had arranged to take lessons four days a week. For six months he had diligently attended. He'd learned to read and write and cypher some. It was the only formal learning he'd ever had, and secretly he was proud of his accomplishment.

As for the vision of loveliness who was indirectly responsible for his higher education, she married her cousin. Such was life, Davy reckoned, as he entered shallow water on the east side of the island.

"Hold on!" Flavius said, alarmed that they were about to go into the water. Twice in the past few days he'd nearly gone to meet his Maker by being dumped in the rightful domain of fish, and he was not inclined to tempt fate a third time. "Don't tell me we have to swim?"

"Take a gander," Davy said, pointing down and moving on. "It's a secret way to the island that only the Ojibwas know. Wawaneechotinka showed it to me."

Flavius bent low. The water at that point was only a few inches deep and clear enough for him to see that a submerged ridge several yards wide linked the island to the mainland. "Well, I'll be!" he said. "I wish I'd known this was here before."

Nervously kneeing the dun forward, Flavius braced himself in case the horse shied or reared. For once the contrary animal behaved, apparently reassured by the presence of the sorrel, and in due course dry ground was under them again. Flavius was as happy as a flea in a doghouse. He hummed as they rode along, calculating how many days it would be before they reached Tennessee.

Although Davy preferred to ride quietly, he did not want to spoil his friend's good mood. Heading to the southeast, he held the horses to a lope that ate up the miles but did not unduly tire them. By noon they were meandering through forested hills. A bald spot on top of one hill was as likely a spot as any to stop and rest.

Davy dismounted and opened a beaded leather bag Tokawonda had given him shortly before they left. In it was enough jerky and other edibles to last them a week. Selecting a strip, he munched hungrily. The dried venison had been flavored, lending it a taste reminiscent of honey.

"Downright delicious," Flavius said, doing the same. His belly had been growling for hours. He patted it, and abruptly realized that there was a lot less of him than there had been when they started on their gallivant. "Appears that I've lost some weight, doesn't it?"

"I'd guess upwards of twenty pounds," Davy said.

"That much?" Flavius ran his hand over his stomach again, then tugged on his shirt to see how loosely it hung. Where once it had fit as snugly as a woman's corset, now there were two inches or better of space between the buckskin and his hide. "I'll be hornswoggled if it ain't true. Matilda will be tickled pink. She's been nagging me for a coon's age to shed some weight."

Davy grinned. "By the time we're home, you'll be as thin as a broom."

"You really think so?"

Movement in a valley west of the hill cut off Davy's response. Snatching the sorrel's reins, he led the horse into the trees, saying, "Take cover. We're not alone."

Flavius darted to the dun. His lunge spooked the high-strung animal into back-stepping away from him. Running after it, he snagged the reins. "Remind me to sell this nag and get a new horse when we get back," he said as he hurried into the shadows.

Davy stepped over to an oak and climbed. Stopping at a fork twenty feet up, he shielded his eyes from the sun. A long line of Indians was passing through the valley in single file. They were too far off for him to be certain, but he suspected they were Fox warriors. It bothered him that they were traveling in the general direction of the Ojibwas' island sanctuary. Coincidence? he wondered. Or had Kiyo Kaga learned where Keekweechiweepinank's people were?

"What do you see?" Flavius called up.

Davy told him. He was about to descend when he spotted another long line of men wending through the hills to the east. More Fox warriors, and they were traveling in the same direction. Combined, there had to be over a hundred involved. This was no ordinary war party. The Fox tribe was committing itself to a large-scale operation.

More troubled than ever, Davy rejoined his friend. "I don't like it, Flavius. I've got a bad feeling that Kiyo Kaga plans to attack the Ojibwa village."

"It's miles from here. You're fretting over nothing."

Davy thought of the laughing children and the venerable warrior who had befriended them. "What if I'm

114

not? We can't just ride off and leave them to be slaughtered."

The prospect of tangling with hostiles again made Flavius's mouth go dry. He was going to say that, yes, they could go their own way, that they owed the Ojibwas nothing, that the smart thing to do was light a shuck for home, when into his head popped a picture of the crippled old woman who had brought him mash every day of his captivity. Then there was Kawaka-tusk, the warrior who had spoken on his behalf at the council. And all those little innocent children. He said nothing.

Davy rubbed his chin while pondering. "As you say, we're miles from the village. Maybe it would be better to shadow the Fox a while and see if they really are heading for the island. If not, we'll go our own way with no harm done."

"Sounds good to me," Flavius said. *Any* plan that did not involve swapping lead and arrows with a war party that size was all right by him.

Mounting, Davy hugged dense cover until he came to the bottom of the hill. Paralleling the band to the west, he stayed in the deep woods where he was less likely to be detected.

An hour elapsed and the Fox warriors did not change course. The two lines were approximately half a mile apart, maintaining the same pace.

Davy wanted to get closer. It was risky, but he had observed that one of the men at the head of the west column seemed to be bound and occasionally stumbled. Announcing his intention to Flavius, he swung off the horse and handed over the reins. "I'll do it on foot. You keep on as you're doing. I shouldn't be long."

Not thrilled at being left alone, Flavius said, "Couldn't we do it together?"

"Doubles the odds of being seen," Davy said. Adjusting his coonskin cap, he sped into the undergrowth, gliding over the ground like a human antelope, making no more noise than a cougar would.

The band to the west was about to enter a gap between two hills. Davy came to a log within a hundred yards of them and crouched. He was just in time. A tall warrior in the lead raised an arm and the line halted.

This close, Davy saw that the leader was none other than Kiyo Kaga. The chief and every other warrior were painted for war as well as armed to the teeth. Kiyo Kaga stalked back to the fourth man, who did indeed have his arms tied behind his back.

It was an Ojibwa! The man's head hung low and there was dry blood on the right half of his face and his right shoulder. His buckskin shirt had been torn, his leggings were ripped. He did not look up when Kiyo Kaga addressed him. For that he was roughly seized, spun around, and brutally cuffed.

Davy put two and two together: A lone Ojibwa hunter had been captured after a struggle and was being forced to lead the hated enemy of their people to the village. But why would the man do it, knowing the consequences?

Kiyo Kaga suddenly drew a knife and poked the captive, who flinched but did not cry out. When Kiyo Kaga received no response to his next statements, he straightened and hollered. From the rear of the line hurried a Fox warrior leading another captive, one Davy had not noticed.

Homecoming

It was a boy of ten or so, undoubtedly the Ojibwa's son. Likewise bound, he bore bruises on his face and neck. Holding his head high in defiance, he was ushered before Kiyo Kaga.

The Fox leader spoke to the father. Once more the man refused to answer. This time Kiyo Kaga grabbed the son by the front of the shirt and held the knife against his throat.

Anguish etched the father's face. The Ojibwa stared forlornly at the boy, then at Kiyo Kaga. Faced with the choice of doing whatever Kiyo Kaga wanted or having his son suffer, the man did what any father would do. He broke. Quickly he responded, bobbing his head to the northwest.

Davy understood. The Ojibwa was giving added directions to the island. In another hour the Fox war party would be there. Unless Keekweechiweepinank was warned, the Ojibwas would not stand a prayer. Taken by surprise, they would be massacred to the last man, woman, and child.

More often than not Indian warfare consisted of small raids and minor skirmishes. Pitched battles were rare. Most tribes were content to indulge in war in much the same way they indulged in hunting and fishing. They never thought in terms of total extermination.

There were exceptions, as there were to every rule. The Hurons had fought ruthlessly to wipe out the Iroquois. The Creeks were equally fierce toward their enemies. And now Kiyo Kaga was about to elevate the Ojibwa-Fox rivalry to new heights of bloodletting and savagery.

Reluctantly Davy crawled into the brush, rose, and

117

jogged off. There was nothing he could do for the father and son. If he trailed the war party in order to try to free them, he would lose precious time needed to reach the Ojibwa village. Mulling his options, he presently caught up with his friend.

Flavius did not hear Davy coming. He was lamenting the fickle whim of perverse fate that had delayed, once again, his return home. Just when things were going right, they had gone all wrong.

The touch of a hand on Flavius's leg almost made him jump out of his skin. He started to swing his rifle around, then saw who it was.

"Davy! Consarn it! You scared me out of ten years' growth! Next time don't sneak up on a body like that!"

"Sorry," Davy apologized, climbing on the sorrel. Relating what he had seen, he concluded with: "We have to warn Keekweechiweepinank. Thing is, I don't like leaving that father and that boy in Kiyo Kaga's clutches. I was at a loss what to do until it hit me."

Flavius squirmed in the saddle. Whenever Crockett used that tone, it invariably spelled trouble. "What did?"

"One of us has to go to the village while the other shadows the war party and waits for a chance to get the captives out of there."

"You want us to separate again?" Flavius said, horror-stricken. "No, no, no. Whenever we do, I wind up regretting it. Let's ride to the village together, then come back for that man and his boy."

"We don't have the time," Davy objected. He had already made up his mind that it was the right thing to do. Checking the position of the sun, he said, "One of us has to leave right this minute. Which one should it be? I'll let you pick."

"Oh, thanks," Flavius said glumly. Some choice. Should he stay and attempt to outwit an entire war party, or should he risk life and limb riding pell-mell to the village? To be honest, he would rather bear the news to the Ojibwas. But to be even more honest, that would be wrong. "Your horse is faster than mine and you're better at finding your way, so you should be the one to go," he admitted.

"Are you sure?" Davy did not have to read minds to know that his friend did not like his idea one bit. "I can lend you my horse. You can warn them."

Flavius would have leaped at the idea, except, as he explained, "I've never ridden the sorrel. It might not like having someone else at the reins and act up." Sighing, he shook his head. "No, it's best if I stay."

Davy put a hand on his friend's shoulder. "Don't take needless risks. It's my bet that Kiyo Kaga will make camp about nightfall and wait until morning to attack. Sometime during the night you should be able to slip on in and release the captives."

"Easy as pie."

There was much more Davy wanted to say, but he let a squeeze of Flavius's shoulder suffice. "Until we meet again," he said, nodding, then jabbed his heels into the sorrel and trotted northward. As the vegetation closed around him he glanced back. Flavius looked heartbroken.

"Everything will be fine!" Davy was tempted to shout, but he did not. For one thing, the wind might carry it to the Fox band to the east. For another, circumstances just might make a liar of him.

Once he was safely out of earshot of the war parties, Davy brought his mount to a gallop. Since he always made it a habit to memorize landmarks as he went along, he had no difficulty retracing his steps. It was not long before the hills were behind him, lowland waterways ahead.

Davy rode like the wind in order to reach the village well in advance of Kiyo Kaga. Keekweechiweepinank needed plenty of time to prepare.

He had gone about halfway when he came to a spot where the trail wound to the right around marshland dotted by reed-covered hummocks and isolated stands of trees. If he were to cut across, he'd save minutes.

Reining sharply, Davy threaded through the hummocks, always on the lookout for snakes and bogs and other perils. The surefooted sorrel had a knack for sticking to the driest, safest strips of ground, so he was not overly concerned about a mishap.

Then a thicket hid the next stretch. Davy swept around a turn and started across a flat space. Without warning the sorrel stumbled and keeled forward. Davy was thrown against its neck, and would have fallen had he not clutched at the saddle. Heaving upright, he discovered that they had blundered into a bog unlike any he'd ever encountered. It was similar to quicksand, only wetter and slicker.

Davy cut to the left and tried to spur the sorrel out. The horse tried its utmost, but the clinging mud weighed it down so that it could barely move. The whole while, they were gradually sinking.

Davy worked the reins as expertly as any man could. He used his legs to full advantage. There was no telling how deep the hole might be. But something told him that if he did not get the sorrel out of there quickly, he would lose it, and maybe his own life besides.

Never once had Davy ever beaten or otherwise mistreated a horse. The closest he came was that very moment when he whipped the sorrel like a man possessed, hurting it for its own sake, seeking to goad it into gaining solid ground before it was too late. He slashed the reins across its neck, across its shoulders, across its face.

Beside itself with confusion and fear, the sorrel made a herculean effort to gain the bank. It hurled itself forward, plowing through the mud, a living battering ram that nearly reached a hummock before the mud brought it up short.

"Just a little further!" Davy urged, applying the reins again. He almost lost his rifle, which he had slipped under his left arm. Holding fast, he inched the horse closer and closer to their mutual salvation.

Davy smiled grimly. They were nearly there! Another few inches and they would be on their way.

The sorrel must have found purchase under the surface because it suddenly shot upward, taking the steep bank in a driving run. Caught off balance, Davy grabbed at its mane so he would not fall. As he did, his rifle slid loose. He had to let go of his mount to snatch it, and in doing so, he lost his perch on the saddle.

Davy flung the rifle from him in midair. He heard it clatter on the bank as he struck the mud. In the final instant, he had the presence of mind to straighten his spine and fling his arms and legs out from his side. It cushioned the impact. It also distributed his weight

David Thompson

more evenly so that instead of being sucked under, he only sank a few inches.

Out of the corner of one eye Davy saw the sorrel scramble to safety. The horse nickered and shook itself, then looked down at him.

"Stay, boy!" Davy called, afraid it would come back in after him. In his position he could not get it out a second time. He lay perfectly still, the mud molding like glue to his buckskins and head but not pulling him under any further. It was a trick that worked in quicksand, so why not here?

The sorrel pranced and tossed its head. It did not like the situation, and twice it made as if to trot down the bank to his side.

"Stay!" Davy repeated. Twisting his neck, he judged that he was only six feet from the bank. But it might as well be a mile. His sole hope was to wriggle out of the mud an inch at a time, yet that would take hours, hours he did not have to spare.

Davy glanced at the bank again. There had to be a faster way. But what? Paddling like a dog would not be practical. The mud was too thick. Nor would sitting up and lunging. He would be up to his waist, or higher, in the blink of an eye.

Seconds ticked by, and all Davy could think of was the Fox war party on the march, drawing steadily closer to the unsuspecting Ojibwas. It would be his fault if they were slaughtered. He'd been given the opportunity to save them and he had botched it.

The thought seared him like a burning arrow.

If there was one thing his father had impressed on him, it was that the Crockett clan were not quitters. An Irishman never gave up. Ever.

Davy moved his shoulders and hips, imitating a snake. The mud rose higher but not high enough to engulf him. He moved toward the bank at a painstaking pace, so slow that it was unbearably aggravating. Gritting his teeth, wriggling harder, he had to abruptly stop when the mud crept up to his ears, some of it sliding under his chin.

Meanwhile the sorrel was shaking itself, throwing gobs of mud every which way. It danced in a circle, its tail hanging limp, a great brown lump.

Davy resumed wriggling, exerting more pressure on his hips than his shoulders. He made quicker headway, but he also sank faster. Mud tickled the holes in both of his ears.

Halting, Davy girded himself. It was all or nothing. Too much was at stake for him to delay any longer. He envisioned Elizabeth and the children, and prayed they would not hold it against him if he never returned. "I'm sorry," he said softly. He had long suspected that his wanderlust would be the end of him, and apparently it would.

Bunching both shoulders, Davy tensed his legs and turned his face to the bank. Five feet. That was all it was. He took a deep breath, thrust both legs down, then hurtled at the slope with his arms outstretched.

Chapter Ten

"I hate this, hate this, hate this."

It was a litany, of sorts. Flavius had said it over and over again since Davy disappeared, and he was still saying it as Kiyo Kaga's band wound down through the hills to the lowland country claimed by the Ojibwas.

Doing as Davy had instructed him, he shadowed the Fox warriors without letting them see him. That posed no problem so long as there was woodland in which to hide, but once Kiyo Kaga left the hills, trees were few and far between. The high grass, tall enough to screen the war party's advance, would not conceal the dun.

Safely screened by maples, Flavius stared after the retreating line until the last warrior vanished. He allowed another couple of minutes before he nudged the dun into the open. Rising in the stirrups, he scanned the grass and did not see the Fox band. It was probably all right for him to go on, he figured.

"I hate this, hate this, hate this," Flavius muttered yet again. He should have accepted Davy's offer and taken the sorrel. So what if it had kicked up a fuss? At least horses were not notorious for carving folks up into tiny pieces, or scalping them, or throttling them with their own guts. All of which the Fox warriors might do if they got their hands on him.

Flavius was so nervous that when blades of grass quivered to his left, he whipped around and jerked up his rifle, prepared to go down fighting. He felt like a fool when a marsh wren zipped into the air.

"A dumb bird," Flavius complained under his breath. Clucking the dun forward, he willed his body to relax. But it was useless. His body had a mind of its own. He was as tightly wound as a steel spring.

Davy had done it to him again, had gone and gotten him into a situation he despised. Sometimes it seemed as if every time he turned around, his friend was asking him to risk life and limb. First they just *had* to save those two women from the war party. Then they just *had* to warn the Chippewas about the raid. Now Flavius just *had* to do what he could to free the captured father and son.

It was too ridiculous for words.

As much as Flavius liked and admired Davy, there were times, such as now, when Flavius could not help but think that his friend was prone to getting carried away when it came to doing what was right.

Some might even say Davy was a mite fanatical in that regard.

Not that Flavius thought they were doing wrong.

Far from it. His conscience would never give him any rest if he did not do something to help Keekweechi-weepinank's people. Sure, they had mistreated him at first, but they had been quick to release him once the chief's sister showed up, proving he was not an enemy.

No, what troubled Flavius was Davy's passion for always doing right *no matter what might happen to them*. The personal cost never seemed to be important, in Davy's eyes. His friend was much too willing to sacrifice the both of them, if that was what it took, to do what Davy saw as right. And that was wrong.

The rustle of grass snapped Flavius fully alert. He did not bring up the rifle this time. Just another dumb bird, he reflected, rising as high as he could to see over the tops of the grass. Hundreds of yards to the north the Fox band was crossing a stream.

Flavius was glad. He was awful thirsty, so when he reached the same spot, he dismounted, knelt, and dipped his hands into the cool water. As he raised a cupped palm to his lips, he sensed rather than heard a whisper of movement behind him. An animal, he told himself. Nevertheless, he casually placed a hand on a pistol and thumbed back the hammer. Pretending to bend for another drink, he spun.

Nothing was there. No wild creature of any kind. No Fox warriors. Just high grass standing ramrod straight.

Sheepishly, Flavius wedged the flintlock under his belt. He was behaving like a jackass. He had to get a grip on himself before he committed a blunder that might cost him his life.

The dun was drinking greedily. Swinging up, Flavius pulled hard on the reins and ventured across the stream. Tracks lined the opposite bank where the war party had emerged.

Flavius plodded into a gap they had made. He was in no great hurry. Davy had advised him to wait until the middle of the night to rescue the captives, and that was exactly what he aimed to do.

Sunset was a long time in coming. The countryside changed little, although streams, ponds, and small lakes became more numerous. It was of interest to Flavius that Kiyo Kaga's band swung around to the west shortly before the sun dipped below the horizon. Evidently, come the dawn, the Fox war party would attack the Ojibwa village in a pincer pattern, half from the west and half from the east. He sure hoped that Davy had warned Keekweechiweepinank, or there would be a slaughter the likes of which no one had seen since the French and Indian wars.

In a woodland copse Flavius left the dun and went on afoot. Cautiously picking through the dense vegetation in the growing darkness, he searched for the Fox camp. Perspiration dotted his brow. His mouth was so dry that it hurt to swallow.

Inside his noggin a small voice shrieked at him to forget the Ojibwas, to get out of there while he could. Why throw his life away for a bunch of people who would not shed a tear on his behalf if he were to be slain? It was not as if they were kin or anything.

He was being an idiot, the voice insisted. He should jump on the dun and light a rag for Tennessee and not look back until he reached his cabin. Crockett be hanged. The man had no right asking him to—

A high-pitched yelp brought Flavius up short. It sounded just like a kid crying out, and it had come from the northwest. Hunched low, placing each foot down as quietly as he knew how, he stalked along until he reached a wide gully.

It was so dark by now, and the gully so well concealed, that Flavius nearly stumbled over the edge, which would have been a catastrophe since the band of warriors under Kiyo Kaga were strung out along the bottom, either seated or reclining, resting until the attack at dawn.

A low cough alerted Flavius just as he parted the grass along the rim. Flattening, he scanned the gully, and gulped. Another step and the war party would have spotted him.

No fire had been built, a precaution since the band was so close to the village. Near the mouth of the gully was Kiyo Kaga, along with a half-dozen strapping warriors and the captives. As Flavius looked on, Kiyo Kaga said something to the father, who refused to respond. As a result, Kiyo Kaga slapped the boy. Again the youngster cried out, and this time was seized by a Fox warrior who clamped a hand over his mouth.

Kiyo Kaga drew a long knife. Slowly placing its razor edge against the boy's throat, he once more addressed the father.

The Ojibwa, proud and resolute until that moment, broke. Nodding at his son, he adopted a pleading tone.

Whatever was said pleased Kiyo Kaga, who shoved the boy to the ground, then cut the rope that bound the father.

A stick was placed in the Ojibwa's hands. Hunkering down, the man ripped grass out by the roots, creating a circle of bare earth about the size of a large pumpkin. Next, he drew in the dirt, noting certain aspects for Kiyo Kaga's benefit.

It had to be a map, Flavius guessed. Possibly the Ojibwa was telling about the submerged ridge that linked the island to the mainland. That was the secret chink in the tribe's armor, the one major weakness the island had, a weakness that might spell their doom.

Armed with the valuable knowledge, the war party would be hard to stop. Kiyo Kaga would throw everything he had into crossing at that point. Bowmen would pin the Ojibwas down, enabling Kiyo Kaga's warriors to reach the island. Fighting would then be man-to-man. As things stood, the Ojibwas would be heavily outnumbered. The outcome, Flavius thought, was a foregone conclusion.

But what would happen if Kiyo Kaga were to die ahead of time?

The tantalizing question tempted Flavius to put a ball into the Fox leader's broad back. Only the certainty that his own life would be forfeit moments later deterred him. Slinking backward until it was safe for him to turn east, he crawled toward the gully mouth.

A turtle would have beaten him in a race.

Flavius was leaving nothing to chance. By carefully bending the stalks and then easing onto them before they could spring back, he soundlessly slid to the top of the eight-foot incline. Here he peeked out to verify the father and son were still there. They were, but the father was once again bound. The son leaned against him, bent by despair.

Kiyo Kaga and six warriors were conferring. Making final plans, Flavius assumed.

Drawing back from the rim, Flavius made himself

comfortable. It was early yet. He had a long wait ahead of him. It was best to rest, but he was too over-wrought to doze off. He contented himself with marking the progress of the stars and the constellations. Never had they moved so slowly. The Big Dipper took forever to make its nightly trek.

By a watch it would have been after two in the morning when Flavius inched to the edge. Most of the warriors appeared to be asleep. A man had been left to keep watch below, and another farther up the gully. Kiyo Kaga himself lay nearest the mouth, a blanket draped over his chest and shoulders.

The Ojibwa father and son were slumped against one another. Exhaustion had taken its toll. The father snored lightly, and the boy's chest rose and fell in rhythmic proof that he was also sound asleep.

Flavius licked his lips. How in tarnation was he to whisk the pair away? If either of the two warriors on guard let out a yell, he would have fifty fierce savages breathing down his neck. Davy had asked the impossible. Going down there was guaranteed to get him killed.

The boy shifted and muttered in his sleep, then whined like a stricken puppy. Dry blood formed a dark stain at the corner of his mouth. Above his left eye was a welt the size of a goose egg.

Damn it all! Flavius reflected. Snaking down the incline headfirst, he relied on his elbows and knees to slow him when gravity tried to take over. At the bottom he crawled to the left, to the opening.

Not five feet away lay Kiyo Kaga.

Flavius wondered what motivated a man like that to do what he was doing. From what Keekweechiweepinank had told Davy, he gathered that the Fox chief wrongly blamed the Ojibwas for the deaths of two of his sons. Rumor had it that the young men had gone off hunting, never to return. Kiyo Kaga had led a party that found their butchered bodies close to the edge of disputed territory, and had leaped to the conclusion that the Ojibwas were to blame.

Keekweechiweepinank had sworn that that was not the case. He had consulted with the heads of other villages, and they'd been unanimous in their belief that Ojibwas had not been responsible. Any of a dozen other tribes might have been the culprits. But convincing Kiyo Kaga of his mistake was as likely as a man walking on the moon. In his grief-stricken lust for vengeance, Kiyo Kaga was hardly in a mood to listen to reason. Nothing short of the total extermination of the Ojibwas would satisfy him.

Flavius squelched an urge to shake violently as he moved closer. He could hear Kiyo Kaga's breathing, could see the guard a few yards beyond. The man's back was to him.

Almost at the chief's elbow, Flavius partially rose. In his mind's eye he saw himself stepping over Kiyo Kaga and bashing the sentry. A second after that he would haul the Ojibwas to their feet and propel them from the gully, shooting the Fox leader or anyone else who attempted to stop them. Once in the grass, he would cut the father and son free so they could run faster. Then all they had to do was get to the dun ahead of the war party, and head for the village.

Simple, right?

Flavius raised his leg to pass Kiyo Kaga. He did not notice the chief move, but suddenly the tip of a knife was gouging his inner thigh. A chill coursed through him. He turned to stone, dumbstruck as Kiyo Kaga straightened and snatched the rifle from his grasp. The knife rose to press against his belly, but did not bury itself in his flesh as he feared.

Kiyo Kaga's hawkish eyes raked Flavius, confusion and disbelief competing for dominance. Flavius knew why. The Fox leader could not understand why a lone white man had appeared out of nowhere. Kiyo Kaga's curiosity was the only reason Flavius had not been killed outright.

At a word from the chief, the guard sprang to his side. So did five warriors who had seemed to be asleep. Flavius was surrounded, stripped of his weapons, and shoved to the ground next to the Ojibwas, who woke up and gawked in astonishment at him. Instead of rescuing them, he was now in the same fix they were. He did not resist as his arms were wrenched behind him and his wrists tied.

Every last Fox was up now. Kiyo Kaga sent warriors out to probe the vicinity. Presently they came back, evidently to report that there was no sign of other white men. Kiyo Kaga stabbed a finger at Flavius and spoke, but all Flavius could do was shake his head.

Meanwhile, the night waned. It would not be long before the war party launched its attack.

Thanks to Davy Crockett, Flavius was caught smack dab in the middle—with no way out.

Hours earlier, the object of Flavius Harris's irritation had thrown himself at the bank surrounding the muddy bog in which he was trapped. As soon as he straightened, his legs sank to the hips. His chest knifed through the mud, but only for a couple of feet. His outstretched hands were shy of firm ground when the bog commenced to suck him under.

"No!" Davy involuntarily called out, and tried again, throwing every iota of strength he had left into a last attempt. His fingers parted the slick quagmire, then the middle three fastened onto something that did not give way. Hanging by his fingernails, he fought the heavy pull. It felt as if his legs weighed a ton each, as if his feet were encased in cement. Heaving upward, he groped for the bank with his other hand. His joy when he found it knew no bounds.

The sorrel watched his antics and fidgeted, but it was content to stay put while he got out on his own.

Davy pulled and pulled, pausing to catch his breath when he grew winded. The only parts of him not sodden with mud were the upper half of his face and his coonskin cap.

Mud hanging onto him like a second skin, Davy heaved and tugged until he clambered out of the mire. For the longest while he was too weak to do more than lie there and thank his Maker for seeing him through alive.

Davy did not know how much time had been lost. Any amount was too much.

Digging his heels in, he flung himself upward. It was a worthy try, but the bank was too steep. Losing his footing, he crashed down and slid, nearly dumping himself into the mud again.

Once was more than enough. Davy would rather take on a pack of rabid dogs—naked and unarmed— than go through that a second time.

Although he wanted to leap to his feet and gallop

off, Davy knew he was not up to it. He did not move until he was recovered enough to brush at the thick brown layers on his arms and legs. The mud would not wipe off; all he did was stir it.

As if his clothes being covered was not bad enough, both pistols, his tomahawk, and his knife were also caked with mud.

Davy picked up his long rifle. With it to keep him from losing his balance, he shuffled to the top. The sorrel thudded its hooves a few times to demonstrate its impatience. Gripping the reins, he tramped on through the marsh until they came to a small pool.

There was no hesitation on his part. Davy leaned his rifle against a sapling and waded right in. The sorrel, though, must have thought he was crazy in light of what they had just been through. It planted itself and would not budge, come what may. He yanked. He coaxed. He cajoled. The sorrel was having none of it.

Exasperated, Davy went out deeper. The water around him turned the color of dirt. He cleaned his buckskins as best he could without taking them off. Venturing into the shallows, he washed off his knife and tomahawk and dried them with handfuls of grass.

The pistols had been rendered useless. Davy broke the end off a low branch and peeled the mud from the flintlocks as if it were the skin of an orange. More valuable time was consumed, but he could not afford to go on unarmed. The two Fox bands he had seen might not be the only ones in the area. Plus there were grizzlies and panthers to think of.

Reloaded and clean, Davy was soon under way. His shortcut had backfired on him, so now he had to make up for lost time. Once out of the marshy tract, he brought the sorrel to a gallop.

Despite the urgency, it was wonderful to fly along with the wind whipping the tail of his cap. It reminded Davy of his childhood, when he had roamed the hills of Tennessee. Those had been deliriously grand days. He'd been as free as a bird, once his chores were done. Every spare moment had been spent hunting and fishing and scampering over hill and dale as if all of creation were his personal plaything.

A log in his path brought Davy back to the here and now. A flick of the reins, and the sorrel vaulted the obstacle as neatly as any of the purebred stock raised by the gentry down to New Orleans.

Landmarks indicated that Davy was nearing the island. Another quarter of a mile and the Ojibwas would learn the bad tidings. What would Keekweechiweepinank do? Davy wondered. Defend the village? Or flee, deserting the island to preserve his people? It was a decision Davy was glad he did not have to make.

A stream had to be forded. Unwilling to hunt for the shallowest part, Davy barged across, spraying water like a fountain. He swept up the other side, passed under a tree, rounded a boulder, and saw a line of warriors in front of him. Too late, Davy attempted to rein up. He was among them in a twinkling. Two of them leaped, catching hold of him around the waist and chest. He resisted, but the next moment he was torn from the saddle.

Chapter Eleven

Davy Crockett was slammed onto his back. He struck with his rifle, the stock smashing one warrior across the shins. Another pressed Davy's shoulders flat while a third hiked a war club to split his skull. Suddenly the man with the club hesitated, his eyes widening.

Davy was snapped to his feet so fast, his teeth crunched together. Bewildered, he was speechless when his hand was warmly clasped by the man who had almost slain him. Over and over the warrior said the same thing. Only then did Davy recognize the men as Ojibwas. The word the warrior was saying was "Friend."

"You've got that right," Davy allowed, offering no objection when his back was clapped and he was guided toward the secret trail to the island. He led the sorrel, which nipped at any Ojibwa that came too close.

Homecoming

Children were frolicking on the shore. Women were busy at a variety of tasks. From wigwams wafted tendrils of smoke. It was a peaceful, idyllic scene, a far cry from what it would be in the morning.

A shout by one of the warriors brought dozens of villagers·on the run. Davy scanned them for a sign of their leader. As he turned from left to right, a lithe figure flew out of the crowd and flung itself at him. Before he could lift a finger, Wawaneechotinka had nearly bowled him over. She threw her arms around his neck and laughed like a little girl just given her heart's desire for her birthday.

"You come back, Red Cheeks! You change your mind! You want me!"

Davy's cheeks grew redder. Prying her arms off him, he said, "You're making a spectacle of yourself."

"If you want me I not care," Wawaneechotinka declared with the bluntness so common to young women naive in affairs of the heart.

"That's just it," Davy said, and paused, seeking words that would let her down easy. There were none. "You've got it all wrong, I'm afraid. I'm here to see your brother. It's urgent."

From out of the crowd strode their tall leader. "What is?" he demanded in that imperious manner of his.

Davy told them. To be sure the chief understood exactly how many Fox were on the march, he flicked his fingers and thumbs up and down ten times. "And there might be more," he cautioned. "This is all-out war. Kiyo Kaga must have rounded up every able-bodied warrior in his tribe. He means to wipe you out and burn your village to the ground."

Keekweechiweepinank's features had darkened as he listened. He was a human storm cloud ready to burst. "All this bloodshed," he said bitterly, "and we not ones who killed his sons. It is wrong."

"What will you do?" Davy inquired.

"What else I do?" Keekweechiweepinank gestured at a cluster of children, then at several elderly Ojibwas. "I have them to think of. They not run fast enough to get away. If we flee, Kiyo Kaga will catch us. In woods we be at his mercy." He surveyed the village. "Here we have chance. We stay and fight."

Davy Crockett had done his duty. He had warned the Ojibwas. Now it was up to them. Since he was not a member of their tribe, he did not have to stay. No one would have held it against him if he skedaddled while he still could. Except himself.

"Count me in," Davy said. "I'd like to lend a hand if you'll have me."

Keekweechiweepinank's flinty gaze softened. "We be honored to have our white brother fight by our side."

The setting sun roosted on the rim of the world, casting a blood-red reflection on the surface of the lake. Davy walked toward the water, noting the thick growth of reeds that choked the shore. "I have some experience in these things," he mentioned. "Are you open to suggestions?"

The Ojibwa leader pointed at strips of deer meat drying on a wooden frame. "You see those?" Shifting, he indicated a pile of wild onions near a wigwam. "And those?" Keekweechiweepinank paused. "My people not like some that live only for war. We be hunters and gatherers. We depend on our Mother for all we need."

"I live off the land too," Davy remarked when the chief stopped, but Keekweechiweepinank did not seem to hear him.

"We defend what is ours. But we happy to be left alone. We not make war unless we have no choice." The leader sighed. "Now we have no choice. So, yes, I listen to your words. Without your help, I fear my people all die."

The statement jarred Davy. It was a terrible responsibility to have thrust on his shoulders. "I'll do what I can," he offered, "but don't get your hopes too high. When I said that I have experience at making war, I wasn't claiming to be an expert. Not by a long shot. I'm not Andy Jackson."

"Who?"

"A general of ours who won a few battles. Of late he's taken to strutting around like a rooster and acting like he's king of the barnyard." Davy saw that Keekweechiweepinank did not understand, so he said, "He's not important. What is, though, is that I can't make you any promises. My help might not be enough to turn the tables on Kiyo Kaga."

"We do best we can. No one can ask more of us."

A tour of the village, including the island's perimeter, occupied them until well after sunset.

Keekweechiweepinank assembled his people and informed them of the impending attack. Davy half expected some of them to be overcome by fear, to have women dashing around screaming and children bawling their brains out. He should have known better. They took the shocking news soberly, then knuckled down to doing what their leader required.

Scores of torches were lit and set up around the island so that there would be light to work by. Keekweechiweepinank directed them, acting on advice that Davy gave, advice born of Davy's participation in the Creek War. The Ojibwas soon picked up on that fact. Now and then when several walked by him, they would smile, their faces lit by hope.

It unsettled Davy. The whole tribe was counting on him to do the impossible. He wanted to get it across to them that he was not their savior, that whether they lived or died depended entirely on them. He just happened to be in the right place at the right time to lend them a hand, was all.

The hours passed quickly. Keekweechiweepinank divided his people into groups and gave each a specific task. Men, women, children, they all had work to do. There was so much that needed doing and too little time in which to get it done.

A few women carried water skins around, giving drinks to those too busy to stop for more than a second or two. Davy was chipping away at the side of the council lodge with his butcher knife when a finger tapped him on the shoulder.

"You be thirsty, Red Cheeks?"

Davy turned. "Reckon I am," he admitted, wiping a sleeve across his forehead. Accepting a birch-bark bowl filled to the brim, he drained it in three gulps, then smacked his lips. "I'm obliged, Wawaneechotinka."

The maiden would not look him in the eyes. Head bowed, she demurely began to leave, but stopped. "There are words I must say, Red Cheeks."

Homecoming

"Can't it wait?" Davy responded, fearing she was about to profess her affection again.

"No." Straightening, Wawaneechotinka said, "I think a lot. About you." Taking a deep breath, she continued in a rush. "I was wrong, Red Cheeks. When woman want man, man must want woman or it not good. I think only of me, not of you. My mother say that wrong. My brother say that wrong. I not think so till now."

"Better late than never, as my kind like to say." He patted her wrist. "No harm done. It'll be for the best anyway. One day a handsome Ojibwa will sweep you off your feet, and before long you'll have more young'uns underfoot than you'll know what to do with."

"You think so?" Wawaneechotinka smiled wistfully. Abruptly stooping, she planted a kiss on his lips before whirling and bounding off like an antelope in flight.

Staring after her, Davy chuckled. A few hours ago she had wanted to ravish him. Now she acted as shy as a schoolgirl with her first crush.

Affairs of the heart could be as comical as they were mystifying. He recalled his first love, and how long it had taken him to recover when she married someone else. In time Wawaneechotinka would outgrow her infatuation with him and get on with the business of living her life.

It was the way of things.

The sound of reeds being chopped down by the lake reminded Davy of the pressing chore he had to finish. Applying the butcher knife to the wigwam, he glanced at the sky. Midnight was not far off. Five or six hours after that, the Fox war party was bound to strike.

Davy hoped that all went well for Flavius. If not, there was nothing he could do. He was committed to stay until after the attack. His friend was on his own.

Flavius Harris watched the Fox band prepare for the raid, and fervently wished he were anywhere other than where he was. His hands were numb from having the circulation cut off for so long. His shoulders ached abominably.

Twice during the night Kiyo Kaga had interrogated him, but since neither knew the other's tongue, they might as well have been deaf and dumb. In anger the leader had cuffed him, and Flavius had taken the punishment without complaint. It beat having a knife thrust between his ribs.

As bad as things were, Flavius had cause to hope: He was still alive. So were the Ojibwa father and son, who likewise had tried to communicate with him, with the same result. Neither knew any English.

It was an hour before dawn when Flavius was startled by the unexpected appearance of three husky figures at the mouth of the gully. The newcomers consulted with Kiyo Kaga, who showed them the crude map drawn in the dirt. After a while the trio melted into the night.

Flavius figured they were from the other half of the war party, come to receive last-minute orders from Kiyo Kaga. The raid was being superbly coordinated. Nothing was being left to chance.

Kiyo Kaga, Flavius had noticed, got little rest. The chief had a haggard look about him, as if he had not slept well in a very long time. In his eyes burned bright flames of hatred for those he believed had slain his sons, especially whenever he sat and stared morosely in the direction of the island.

Flavius had tried to catch a glimpse of it, but a belt of trees intervened. He guessed that the village was half a mile away, maybe a bit more. Once he thought that he glimpsed pinpoints of flickering light, but it had to be a trick of his tired eyes.

As dawn approached, Flavius grew nervous. If his captors were going to kill him and the father and son, they would do the deed before they headed out.

Soon the warriors were on their feet. Some tested bowstrings. Some honed blades. A warrior with a lance took practice throws at the bank. A few did shuffling dances while standing in place. One or two chanted softly.

An undercurrent of rising excitement crackled in the gully. Kiyo Kaga paced like a caged bear. When a faint glow lit the eastern horizon, he barked commands. The warriors formed into a column behind him.

But not all of them. Two burly specimens with muscles of iron hoisted Flavius to his feet. Another prodded the father and son erect with the tip of his knife.

This is it, Flavius thought. His life was done. He started to mentally recite the Lord's Prayer, only getting as far as "Thy will be done" when he was roughly shoved into step with the rest of the war party as they filed from their hiding place.

Flavius was stunned. Kiyo Kaga was keeping them alive! But why? To torture later? The boy started to struggle and complain, and was immediately gagged. So was the father. A warrior holding a strip of leather by both ends moved toward Flavius. As docile as a little lamb, he let them do as they wanted.

Then the war party picked up speed, fanning out as they entered the woods. Human specters, they flitted across the ground with nary a noise. A man who accidentally stepped on a twig drew a withering glance from Kiyo Kaga.

Flavius and the captive Ojibwas were kept close to the chief. Soon the island appeared through the trees. Not a soul was abroad, although smoke curled from a handful of wigwams. The women would be rousing to begin the morning meal while the rest of their families enjoyed a few extra minutes of sleep.

Worry gnawed at Flavius. Everything was just as it should be, and yet it should *not* be. Davy was supposed to have warned the Ojibwas. Where were the warriors? Why was no one standing guard?

The band veered eastward, toward the spot where the submerged ridge connected to the mainland. Flavius spotted figures gliding toward it from the opposite direction. His hopes soared until he realized the figures were the other half of the war party.

Having been a captive in the Ojibwa village for three days, Flavius knew their routine well. Soon early risers would venture to the lake to wash themselves. Women would fill water skins. Children would scamper out to play before breakfast.

The Fox warriors flowed along the bank that bordered the secret trail. Flavius prayed that one of the Ojibwas would step outside and spot them, but no one appeared. Nor were any dogs roaming about, for once.

Kiyo Kaga was in the lead. He was almost to the spot where the bank sloped down to the underwater ridge.

Homecoming

Flavius pushed at the leather strip with his tongue. Something had gone wrong. Obviously Davy had failed to warn Keeweechiweepinank. So it was up to him. He had to loosen the gag to holler.

The sky brightened rapidly, too rapidly to suit Kiyo Kaga. He gestured sharply, and the Ojibwa father was hustled forward. Kiyo Kaga motioned again. The father looked at his son, then at the village. Kiyo Kaga was impatient. Seizing the boy, he raised his war club. The threat had worked before. It worked again.

The father walked into the water, bending low. Locating the ridge, he moved a few feet out, proving to the Fox that it could be done.

Kiyo Kaga pushed the boy at a warrior and waded out. A wicked grin was eloquent testimony to his thoughts. Victory would soon be his. His sons would be avenged.

A warrior shoved Flavius down the bank and into the lake. Flavius was working at the gag with teeth and tongue, but the leather resisted. He scoured the village again, yearning for someone to pop out and give the alarm. Yet the Ojibwas slumbered on, blissfully unaware of their impending doom.

As Flavius hunched over to better see the ridge, a curious notion sprouted. He glanced at the village again. Something was not quite right. What it was, though, eluded him. A jab in the back moved him forward. At that moment he observed a long line of reeds on both sides of the submerged ridge, from about the middle clear out to the island, reeds that he would have sworn had not been there the day before when Davy and he had crossed.

Flavius was given no time to ponder the mystery.

The same warrior who had shoved him down the bank now shoved him further along the ridge. Flavius took the hint and hurried.

Kiyo Kaga was well ahead, his war club cocked, his other arm fastened around the neck of the Ojibwa father. The Fox leader was using the man as a shield. Shifting from side to side, Kiyo Kaga insured that no arrow or lance could reach him without piercing the hapless captive first.

Flavius looked back. Another warrior was making similar use of the boy. He counted himself lucky that he had not been grabbed. No sooner did he think that, than the warrior behind him locked a brawny arm around his neck.

Flavius reacted instinctively by trying to duck clear of the man's arm. Inadvertently, he stumbled to the left. The warrior snared him, but by then Flavius's foot had slipped off the ridge. He frantically tried to regain his balance. To his dismay, the added pressure and weight against his back tipped him over. He knifed into the lake headfirst.

Panic trampled Flavius's thoughts, reducing him to a terror-filled wreck. *Not again!* Twisting, he sought the surface. The lack of light baffled him, rendering the water equally dark everywhere. Jerking furiously at the cord that bound his wrists, he kicked in one direction, then in another. His shoulder cracked against an object he could barely make out. Dazed, he paused. Which way was up? he wondered desperately.

Already his lungs were near to bursting. He had been taken unaware by the plunge, and had not sucked in a deep breath before going under. He thrashed to the right, thrashed to the left.

146

Homecoming

Flavius wanted to scream in frustration. He bumped against something and flapped his legs so he could swing around and see what it was. As he did, fingers clamped onto his hair and yanked. He would have yelped if he had been above water.

Like an exhausted fish, Flavius was hauled out of the lake and unceremoniously dumped onto his knees on the ledge by the warrior who had caused him to fall. He greedily sucked in air, making too much noise to suit his captors. At a whispered growl from Kiyo Kaga, the warrior drove a foot into Flavius's ribs.

The pain was unbelievable.

Flavius doubled over, his face getting wet again. Sputtering and shaking, he did his best to keep quiet as he was jerked erect and battered toward the village. An arm as stout as hickory closed on his windpipe, nearly forcing him to lose consciousness.

Everything was a blur. Flavius sagged, too weak to manage on his own. The warrior had to practically carry him.

Taking stock, Flavius was surprised to find that the gag had slipped partially off his mouth. Better yet, all that thrashing had loosened the soaked cord binding his wrists. Not by much, but enough that he could move them. Given time, he might be able to free himself.

Time, however, was a luxury he did not have.

Kiyo Kaga was nearing the island. The closer the chief came, the more wary he grew. Although much larger than the Ojibwa, he bent so that the only part of his body exposed to enemy fire was his arm around the man's neck.

The Fox chief was acting just like a real fox about

147

to sneak into a chicken coop, and Flavius couldn't blame him. By now even the rest of the warriors were aware that something was amiss. The village was *too* quiet. There should be Ojibwas moving about, yet there were none. If not for the smoke wafting from several wigwams, anyone with any common sense would have concluded that the village was deserted.

Flavius prayed that it was. He prayed that Davy had gotten through after all, and that Keekweechiweepinank had rounded up the Chippewas and fled into the forest. Maybe they had been able to dig in, to fortify themselves, so when the Fox war party caught up, as it was bound to do, they could give as good as they got.

It would be poetic justice if the Ojibwas kicked the stuffing out of the Fox warriors.

At that juncture all of Flavius's dreams were shattered by a dog that waltzed out of a wigwam and ambled down to the lake to drink. If a dog was there, the Ojibwas must be too. They would hardly go off and leave their animals.

Every member of the war party froze. Bowmen trained arrows on the mongrel, but awaited their leader's signal to fire.

Flavius quivered with anticipation. Bark, damn you! he wanted to bellow. Let your masters know that their enemies are almost on top of them!

The dog lapped a few moments, then looked up. It saw Kiyo Kaga and those behind him. But instead of voicing a warning, it resumed drinking, unconcerned by their presence.

Flavius would have shot the dog himself if he had a gun. The animal finished and pattered back to the wigwam, pausing once to stare at the war party. Stupid cur! Flavius fumed.

Kiyo Kaga waited a bit, then waved his men on. From a wigwam close to the shore fluttered the musical lilt of a woman humming. It brought Kiyo Kaga to a halt just as he stepped onto the island. Listening a few seconds, he spun the Ojibwa father around while simultaneously bringing his war club down on the man's head. The father collapsed without uttering a sound.

It drove the son into a frenzy. Kicking and twisting, he attempted to slip the grasp of the warrior holding him. The man held on, pressing a hand over the gag, and when they came to the island he clubbed the boy with the thick bone hilt of a long knife.

Father and son were left lying side by side.

Flavius assumed that his turn was next. He steeled himself for the blow as he was hustled into the shadows. Warrior after warrior passed him to gather around Kiyo Kaga. Ten. Twenty. Thirty. The submerged ridge was packed with more. The rest waited their turn on the opposite bank.

The warrior holding Flavius slackened his hold. Flavius took that as the cue he was about to be knocked out, or worse. Lifting his legs, he dropped like a rock, bruising his nose when the warrior tried to snag him. He landed on his backside and brought his knees to his chest. The warrior swung a war club aloft.

At that very instant a strident war whoop rent the morning chill, and all hell broke loose.

Chapter Twelve

Davy Crockett had been in the cold water for hours. Long since, the tingling in his legs had ended. They were now numb from the hips down, and he was leery of putting his full weight on them for fear they would not support him.

Not quite as troubling were his shoulders, which were sore from holding a wooden latticework laced with reeds for so long. The circular frame was not all that heavy, but having to keep it perfectly still so that the Fox warriors did not catch on to his ruse taxed him to his limits.

Besides all that, it was unnerving to have enemy after enemy pass within three feet of him, and not do anything.

Davy never knew when one of them might bump the frame, causing it to tilt, or when one might try to peer between the closely threaded reeds to learn what was behind them.

It upset him terribly to have to stand there motionless, his knees braced against the rough side of the submerged ridge, while poor Flavius was being struck and pushed. Yet he dared not act until the pre-agreed moment. At least half the war party must be on the island when he gave the signal.

His heart had leaped into his throat when Flavius fell into the lake. He knew his friend could not swim, and had feared the Fox warriors would let him drown. Fortunately, Flavius had made such a ruckus, the warriors had had to haul him out or risk alerting the enemies they assumed did not know they were there.

Another shaky moment had been when Kiyo Kaga forced the captive Ojibwa father to show him exactly where the submerged route lay. The Ojibwa had stared toward the island first, and could not help but have noticed the new growth of reeds that had miraculously sprouted up on both sides of the ridge.

Davy had fretted that the man might somehow spill the beans. The father, though, had proven that even though he had led the enemies of his people to the island, deep down he was still loyal to his tribe. He had not given anything away.

Davy wondered how the twenty-two Ojibwas in the lake with him were faring. Eleven were on either side, each hidden by a reed latticework similar to his. They were armed either with war clubs or knives or both. He had only his knife and tomahawk. To keep his guns from getting wet and fouling when he needed them most, he had secreted the rifle and both pistols beside the wigwam nearest the water.

Soon it would be time, Davy mused. He saw Kiyo Kaga and other warriors gain the island. Outraged, he watched as the father and son were rendered unconscious. Then a warrior tried to do the same to Flavius and Flavius resisted. There was a tussle. Davy wanted to spring to his friend's aid, but only thirty or forty Fox had crossed. He was supposed to wait until at least fifty did.

Flavius wound up on his back. The warrior elevated a war club. Would the Fox knock Flavius out or bust his skull? It was a question Davy was unwilling to trust to the fickle whims of fate. Throwing back his head, he voiced a Creek war whoop. At the same moment, he whipped the frame holding the reeds up over his shoulders and hurled it at the closest Fox warrior.

All along the ridge, the Ojibwas who had volunteered to conceal themselves in the lake were doing as Davy did. The Fox war party was caught flat-footed. Those who happened to be crossing bore the brunt, many toppled by hurled frameworks. For a few seconds chaos reigned.

Davy beat the Ojibwa warriors out of the water. Grasping the edge, he levered himself onto the ridge, staying on his knees since he did not yet trust his legs. In his other hand was his tomahawk, which he sliced upward, catching a Fox warrior across the stomach, shearing the abdomen wide open. The man shrieked, clutched at the organs spilling out, and went down, sinking swiftly.

Combat erupted all along the ridge. The element of surprise gave the Ojibwas an initial advantage. They disposed of fourteen of their enemies with the loss of just one of their own before the Fox band rallied. Fox warriors on the far bank streamed across to help their friends. Those who had already set foot on the island turned to race back.

Flavius saw those nearest to him start to run to the rescue. The man who had been about to bash in his forehead forgot all about him in the heat of the moment. Temporarily ignored, he wriggled backward until he bumped into a small boulder.

Most of the Fox men on the island were about to pile onto the ridge when Kiyo Kaga's roar stopped them cold. The Fox leader gestured at the wigwams and thundered commands. His followers spread out, several converging on the dwelling where just a few moments ago a woman had been humming.

Dismayed at the thought of an innocent family being slaughtered, Flavius struggled to sit up. He had been working his hands back and forth, but the cord was not yet loose enough for him to slip free.

Two warriors were almost to the entrance when they halted in midstride, as if they had walked into an invisible wall. Flavius did not comprehend why until one of them did a slow pirouette to the ground. Jutting from the man's chest was a feathered shaft.

More arrows streaked from narrow slots made in the side of the wigwam. Another Fox fell. Others retreated out of range.

From the council lodge rose a war whoop. Through the entrance spilled Keekweechiweepinank and a knot of Ojibwa warriors. They were met by Kiyo Kaga and about an equal number of Fox men. Screams and yells mingled in an earsplitting chorus. Arrows flew. Lances streaked. War clubs and knives flashed. In the blink of an eye the tranquil island was transformed into a raging melee.

Flavius heaved and strained. He had to get loose to help! At the moment the Ojibwas were holding their own, but that would change if the rest of the Fox war party reached the island. Already those left on the opposite side were pouring across the underwater ridge. The only thing holding them back was Davy and his small bunch. How long could they hold out?

Davy Crockett was asking himself the same thing. Five of the Ojibwas were down. They had sacrificed their lives gallantly, and those still alive were selling theirs just as dearly, but it would not be enough. There were simply too many of their enemies. For every one the Ojibwas slew, two more rushed forward to take his place. Bodies splashed into the lake or were left sprawled across the ridge.

It helped that the ridge was narrow. Only two or three Fox men could advance at the same time. But it also limited the number of Ojibwas who bore the brunt of the attack. Bit by bit, yard by yard, the Ojibwas were driven back.

Davy was in the middle of the Ojibwa line. At the rate it was going, he figured that over half of the Ojibwas would be dead by the time they reached the shore. Recognizing a losing proposition when he saw one, he motioned for the Ojibwas to fall back. "We'll make our stand at the water's edge!" he shouted, knowing that few of them would savvy a single word. Just so they got his drift.

154

They did. Fighting every inch of the way, the defenders retreated.

Davy halted the instant he stepped from the lake. Facing the oncoming war party, he gestured at the Ojibwas, who promptly formed a living wall between the invaders and the village. In a savage rush the Fox warriors closed. The metallic scrape of steel on steel mingled with the heavy thud of war clubs and the shrieks of the stricken.

It was like the Creek War, only worse. Much worse. Davy had never known battle so fierce. The Ojibwas, defending their home, fought like men possessed. The Fox warriors, determined to exterminate their enemies, were endowed with the ferocity of grizzlies.

Blood flowed as freely as ale at a tavern. Puddles of it dotted the grass, darkened the water. It caked the dead, pulsed from the dying, speckled the living caught in the spray of crimson fountains. The smell of it filled a man's nose, smothering all else.

A Fox reared out of the gloom, a war club hefted for a downward swing. Davy skipped aside in the nick of time, pivoted, and sank his butcher knife into the man's chest. The warrior backpedaled, tottered, then smacked into the shallow water, his eyes as blank as a schoolmarm's empty blackboard.

There was no respite. As soon as one Fox fell, another pounced. Davy retreated under the brutal onslaught of a warrior twice his size. The man wielded a war club with both hands, flailing without cease. Sooner or later he would connect unless Davy did something.

Feinting to the right, Davy went left. It was supposed to trick the Fox into overextending himself so

155

he would be easy pickings. But Davy's foot slipped on a patch of blood. His knee banged hard and he looked up to see his foe poised for the kill.

From out of nowhere whizzed a glittering arrow. It impaled the Fox warrior high in the chest, punching him rearward. He looked down at it, then at Davy, bewilderment snuffed by the rapidly fading spark of life.

Davy's salvation was short-lived. Yet another Fox hurtled at him, this one thrusting a lance that almost sheared into Davy's torso. Davy parried with the tomahawk, parried again with his knife. He tried to stab his adversary, but the Fox skipped beyond arm's length, then barreled in again. The lance afforded the man a greater reach, and he was crafty enough to take full advantage.

Davy ducked. He dodged. He focused on the lance to the exclusion of all else. Another thrust was aimed at his neck, which he countered by swatting the tip with the tomahawk. He was holding his own when the Fox warrior pumped his arm to throw.

Once more a buzzing shaft streaked in out of the blue. This one sliced into the base of the warrior's throat. The man snorted like a stuck bull, gushing blood from his nose and mouth. Refusing to give up, he coiled to spring. Another arrow brought him down.

Davy looked around. It had to be more than coincidence that twice in a row an archer had saved him. He had only seconds to spare, but it was enough.

Standing by the nearest wigwam, bow in hand, was Wawaneechotinka. She smiled at him as she notched another shaft given to her by her mother.

Allowing a few women to remain in the village had

not been Davy's idea. Keekweechiweepinank had insisted, in order to lull Kiyo Kaga into thinking that all the women and children were present. The handful who stayed had been instructed to sing or hum or pretend to talk to others, just as they would do on any ordinary morning. Under no circumstances, though, were any of the women to step outside.

Only two dogs had been left in camp. One was so old that it could barely get around; the other was the one that had gone down to the lake to drink. Years ago it had tangled with a wolverine and had had its neck ripped to ribbons. Somehow the dog had survived, but it could no longer bark or howl or even growl.

A frightened yell by Wawaneechotinka reminded Davy that he had better concentrate on staying alive. He countered a knife speared at his face, danced to one side, and traded a flurry of stabs and thrusts with a sinewy Fox warrior whose skill with a blade was exceptional. Too quick for the eye to follow, they struck, blocked, and evaded one another until the warrior slashed high just as Davy slashed low. The Fox missed. Davy didn't.

Flavius Harris saw his friend triumph, and smiled. His hands were almost loose. Another few seconds and he could join in. He flipped onto his side and bent his neck to see his wrists, then stiffened as a swarthy shape materialized beside him.

A painted Fox warrior, his face was spattered with scarlet drops, drove a war club at Flavius's head. Flavius rolled, and kept on rolling, always in motion, hearing thump after thump as the warrior missed again and again. But not by much. A blow glanced off his shoulder. Another grazed an elbow.

The very next moment Flavius rolled up against a wigwam. He was trapped! There was nowhere to go! Aghast, he saw the warrior tense for the kill.

Above the din, a shot rang out. The warrior's forehead exploded in a shower of flesh, bone, and gore. He sank slowly, the club sliding from limp fingers.

Flavius tried to get out of the way, but the man landed on top of him. Past the warrior's shoulder he spotted Davy, who was lowering a smoking pistol. "Thanks, partner!" he hollered, the cry lost in the uproar.

More and more members of the Fox war party had reached the island. While some engaged the defenders at the end of the ridge, many others had swung wide around them in a flanking maneuver that resulted in the defenders being beset on several fronts at once.

All this while, in the heart of the village Keekweechiweepinank and his warriors were locked in rampaging combat with Kiyo Kaga. Their conflict swirled among the wigwams, the battle ebbing and flowing as circumstance dictated. One minute Keekweechiweepinank and his men were prevailing, the next the tide had turned and they were being hard pressed. Bodies littered the earth. So did discarded weapons.

Davy had darted to his guns with a specific purpose in mind. It had occurred to him that if he could slay the Fox leader, the rest might take it as a bad omen and flee. He'd witnessed the same thing during the Creek War. Apparently, Indians everywhere regarded the death of a leader as bad medicine.

Homecoming

Now, shoving the spent pistol under his belt, he picked up the other flintlock and Liz. As he spun around, an enemy warrior charged. He fired from the hip. A cloud of smoke briefly hid the warrior. It was whisked away by the wind, revealing the man was on the ground, convulsing violently.

Davy wedged the second pistol under his belt. He'd rather reload both, but more was at stake than his personal safety. Running around the wigwam to a point where he could see the two leaders, he raised his rifle and took a bead on Kiyo Kaga.

Just as Davy was about to stroke the trigger, an Ojibwa stepped into the line of fire. Davy shifted for a clearer shot, but the same thing happened again. And again. Each time he took aim, someone spoiled it. The only way he was going to bring Kiyo Kaga down was by throwing himself into the swirl of battle and getting close enough that he could not possibly miss.

Every second of delay added to the cost in lives. Davy barged into the middle of the frenzied conflict, driving the rifle's butt against the temple of a Fox warrior who barred his path. Striking to either side, he angled toward his quarry.

Kiyo Kaga was fighting a thin Ojibwa armed with a broken lance. Repeatedly the Ojibwa spiked the point at Kiyo Kaga, who deftly deflected it with his war club. When the Ojibwa thrust too far, overextending himself, Kiyo Kaga took advantage. The war club caved in the crown of the man's cranium as if it were so much paper.

Davy was twenty-five feet from the Fox chief. The sky had brightened to where he could see the sheen of sweat on Kiyo Kaga's face as he sighted down the bar-

159

rel. His thumb curled the hammer back. The front
sight steadied and the rear sight aligned perfectly.

A fraction of a heartbeat before Davy applied pressure to the trigger, he was rammed into from behind.
It was like being run over by a bull moose. He went
flying in one direction and the rifle went flying in another.

Stunned, Davy sprawled onto his stomach. Around
him swirled the struggling combatants. A foot
brushed his head. Another tromped on his left wrist.
Racked by pain, he pushed onto his hands and knees,
shaking his head vigorously to clear it, uncertain of
who or what had hit him.

Davy knew he had to regain his feet before an en-
terprising Fox warrior finished him off. Rising unsteadily, he was nearly overcome by dizziness. A groan
escaped his lips as he fought to steady himself.
Through the haze that enveloped him one sound rose
above the bedlam. It was a high-pitched scream, torn
from a woman's throat, and it was his name that she
was screaming.

Glancing up, Davy saw a bowman sighting down a
shaft, squarely at his chest. Automatically, he reached
for a pistol, then remembered that both were empty.
Pivoting on the balls of his feet, he tried to throw himself out of harm's way. He was woefully slow.

Smirking, the Fox warrior let fly. The shaft zipped
toward Davy like a dragonfly toward its prey, a blur
against the background of brightening eastern sky.

It all happened so incredibly fast. Davy had no time
to duck or throw up his arms or do anything other
than die. Yet at the same second that the arrow would
have transfixed his body, a figure threw itself in front

of him. He glimpsed long hair, a buckskin dress. The shaft meant to claim his life thumped into the woman instead, jarring her off her feet and into his arms.

Fear eating at him like termites devouring wood, Davy sagged, bearing her gently to the ground. Her head rested in the crook of his elbow. It swayed toward him, and he saw her features clearly. Shock eclipsed the fear, and although his sense of self-preservation made him want to leap to his feet and seek cover before a Fox warrior pounced, he sat there, mesmerized, the same word echoing over and over in his mind. "Why? Why? Why?"

It was Wawaneechotinka's mother, not the maiden. The arrow had skewered her heart, then ruptured out her back. A trace of a smile tweaked her mouth.

"Why?" Davy said aloud, at a loss to explain her self-less act. They had hardly known one another. What reason could she have had for throwing herself in front of him at the fatal instant? To keep her daughter from doing so?

Davy looked up. Wawaneechotinka was fifteen feet away, as dumbfounded as he, her bow slack at her side, her eyes moistening quickly.

South of them the battle was reaching its apex. Ojibwa and Fox warriors were locked in life-and-death struggles. By now every member of the Fox war party able to do so had reached the island. It was the crucial juncture that would decide whether the Ojibwas survived or perished, the moment that Davy had advised Keekweechiweepinank to wait for before committing the Ojibwas held in reserve. Leaping onto a log, Keekweechiweepinank screeched like a red hawk at the top of his lungs.

Wigwams disgorged more Ojibwas. Anxious to help their fellows, howling like ravenous wolves, they flew into the thick of the battle. In a span of less than a minute the advantage shifted to the Ojibwas, and did not shift back. Men fell on both sides, but now more Fox warriors were prone than Ojibwas. Slowly but inevitably the defenders ringed the raiders and forced them toward the lake. Though fighting continued, it was only a matter of time before the attackers were driven off.

Davy was worried about Flavius. Lowering Tokawonda, he started to rise. A gasp and a feral snarl was the only warning he had that at least one member of the Fox war party had not forgotten about Wawaneechotinka or him.

Kiyo Kaga had her by the throat. His war club was gone, but in its place he grasped a bloody knife. He snarled again as if daring Davy to do something so he would have an excuse to sink the cold steel into her bosom.

As still as a rock, Davy was helpless to prevent Kiyo Kaga from using Wawaneechotinka as a shield, just as he had the captive earlier. The bow was wrested from her grip and cast down. When she fought back, Kiyo Kaga nearly tore her hair out by the roots. Wawaneechotinka quieted, but she did not like it.

Davy's rifle was gone. His pistols were empty. He still had his tomahawk and knife, both next to worthless unless he got a lot closer. He stalked them, alert for an opening.

Kiyo Kaga was in a hurry. He threaded through the fray with deceptive ease. Ojibwas who spotted him were stopped in their tracks by the sight of the knife scraping Wawaneechotinka's skin. It did not take long for Kiyo Kaga to reach the canoes. Two other Fox warriors were in the act of pushing one out into the lake. At a word from him they boosted Wawaneechotinka into it, then all three climbed in.

If it was the last thing Davy ever did, he was not going to let Kiyo Kaga escape. Drawing his tomahawk, he darted into the mad whirlwind of battle-crazed enemies. Right away a lance nearly took out an eye. A swipe of his tomahawk drove the Fox warrior back. The man balanced for another try, but an Ojibwa piled into him first.

Kiyo Kaga was on his knees, Wawaneechotinka propped against him. The other two lifted paddles and began to swing the canoe around.

A cry that resembled the screech of a panther more than any human sound split the tumult like a cleaver splitting raw meat.

Keekweechiweepinank had seen his sister being spirited off. Heedless of his own safety, he sprinted toward the lake, shoving aside anyone and everyone who got in his way. Fellow Ojibwas tried to keep up with him, in vain.

Somehow Keekweechiweepinank reached the shore unhurt. He grabbed the end of a canoe and began to push it into the water. He never saw the blood-streaked Fox warrior who bounded toward him.

Davy did. He yelled, but he could not be heard above the clamor.

Keekweechiweepinank almost had the canoe in the water when the Fox behind him arced a knife at the center of his back. Suddenly the canoe lurched to a stop, snagged by rough ground. It threw the Ojibwa leader forward, and the blade intended for his heart cut into his side instead. Glancing off his ribs, it inflicted a severe wound but missed his vital organs.

Keekweechiweepinank tried to rise to face his foe. His hand slipped on the blood pumping from his wound.

The Fox warrior snaked the knife on high for another try. Five bows twanged. Five arrows thunked into the man, front and back. Bristling with shafts, he tottered, tripped over his own feet, and crashed to the bare earth.

Ojibwas surrounded their leader, helping him to stand. By then Davy was there. No one paid him any mind, so without a word he bent and pushed the canoe into the water. Vaulting into it, he scooped up a paddle and set out to save Wawaneechotinka.

"Wait, friend!" Keekweechiweepinank called. Supported by another, he weakly raised a hand.

Davy had no intention of stopping, and no time for jawing. He waved, then stroked briskly, cleanly, propelling the canoe across the lake toward the mouth of a stream. That was where Kiyo Kaga was headed.

A golden glow framed the eastern horizon. Blue sky had replaced the inky starry vault of night. In a short while the sun would rise, so as long as Davy kept the other canoe in sight, he would not lose them.

There was only one problem. Two men could paddle twice as fast as one. But the other canoe bore extra weight, so maybe Davy could hold his own if he paced himself and did not fall too far behind. Kiyo Kaga swept into the stream and was hidden by high reeds. Just as Davy came to the same spot, he glanced back at the village and saw Flavius and two Ojibwas climbing into a canoe.

The stream meandered in a winding course down the valley. At times Davy could see the Fox warriors. At other times his view of them was obstructed by reeds or either bank. He maintained a steady stroke, wary of taxing himself too greatly and faltering later on. Too much was at stake.

On both shores birds broke into their morning chorus. Deer drank along the stream's edge. Now and again a fish would leap out of the water.

Davy was too engrossed in the chase to appreciate the verdant paradise. He had eyes only for the other canoe. Several times the Fox warriors looked over their shoulders, gauging how close he was. They were pacing themselves as well. They did not gain ground and he did not lose any.

Davy would have given anything to have his rifle along. Picking off the Fox warriors would have been as simple as breaking bottles. He negotiated a bend and saw their canoe sweep around another turn forty yards ahead. Arching his spine to relieve a cramp in his lower back, he diligently paddled on.

Around the next bend the stream temporarily narrowed. Across it a patriarch of the forest had fallen, an immense fir tree uprooted by one of nature's temper tantrums. At its base it was as big around as his cabin, if not bigger. One end of the tree rested on each bank.

Davy started to slow, then saw that there was ample space underneath for him to pass. He veered toward a point where the limbs had broken off and ducked so he could slip through the gap unhindered. Its shadow fell across him. For several seconds he glided in a twi-light realm, the bole of the forest giant a mere hand's width above his head.

Bent down as he was, Davy could see that past the tree the stream turned yet again, this time to the north. The other canoe was nowhere in sight. He figured that it had already gone around the bend, and as he sailed out from under the fir, he raised his paddle to resume the pursuit.

Davy would never know what made him glance up. He did not hear anything. Nor did he detect movement above him. But glance up he did, to discover one of the Fox warriors perched on the stub of a thick limb, close to the trunk. In the warrior's mouth was the hilt of a knife, which he grabbed as he pushed off from the tree and swooped toward Davy like a bronzed bird of prey.

Davy swung the paddle as the man alighted in the stern. It clipped the warrior on the shoulder, not hard enough to knock him out of the canoe but hard enough to cause the canoe to tilt violently. Both of them had to grip the side to keep from being dumped into the water.

The Fox recovered first and sprang, cold steel gleaming bright in the morning sunlight.

At a disadvantage because his back was to his foe, Davy twisted and lanced the paddle at the man's chest. The warrior shifted to sidestep, but there was not enough room. The paddle caught him in the sternum. Before he could grab anything, he pitched overboard.

Davy stuck the paddle in the stream and commenced to pump his arms to get out of there. To his consternation, he saw the other canoe abruptly swing around the bend and zip toward him. Kiyo Kaga was coming back! The wily Fox leader had no intention of letting him get out of there alive.

Suddenly Davy's canoe shook and swayed. The first warrior was attempting to clamber back in. Davy brought the paddle crashing down on one of the man's hands—the hand holding the knife. Knuckles burst, bones cracked, and the blade disappeared in the stream.

Snarling viciously, the Fox warrior let go and treaded water. He glared spitefully, then lashed out with his right leg, kicking the canoe. It swung a few feet to one side. The man kicked it again, sneering broadly, as if what he was doing was unspeakably clever.

Davy thought it stupid. It accomplished nothing. He leaned over and went to straighten the canoe. That was when an outcry from Wawaneechotinka snapped his head up. In a twinkling he realized how wrong he was. The warrior had indeed been clever. For now his canoe was nearly broadside, and bearing down on it at top speed was Kiyo Kaga's. He dipped the paddle in, managing a single stroke before impact.

The high-ended bow of Kiyo Kaga's canoe rammed into the side of Davy's, missing him by a few inches. It sheared clean through and out the other side. Birch bark splintered, chips of wood flying everywhere.

Immediately, Davy felt water spurt over his legs. He heaved to his feet. So did Kiyo Kaga and the other warrior. Kiyo Kaga had the knife, the second man a war club. Davy met them with his tomahawk in hand.

Since Ojibwa canoes were only a foot and a half wide, it was hard for a man to keep his balance. The warrior with the club found that out when he delivered a powerful blow that Davy evaded. Unable to check his swing, the warrior stumbled, exposing his head and neck.

Davy imbedded the tomahawk above the man's right ear. He yanked on the handle to free it, but the steel was caught fast in the man's skull. A sizzling stroke of Kiyo Kaga's knife made him relinquish his grasp. It was either that or lose his hand.

Drawing his own knife, Davy crouched. His canoe was sinking swiftly. His sole hope lay in carrying the fight to the Fox chief, and with that in mind he leaped for the bow of the other canoe.

Kiyo Kaga was anticipating the move because he took a step when Davy was in midair, his blade arcing in an underhand thrust.

Davy was helpless to avoid it. He braced for the searing anguish that would burn through his chest into his heart. Only there was none.

At the last moment Wawaneechotinka threw herself at Kiyo Kaga's legs. Slammed off balance, he flapped his arms like an ungainly bird, trying to recover.

Davy did not let him. He slashed once. Twice. Three times. The Fox leader's shirt parted. So did his throat and abdomen. Futilely trying to hold back the deluge of scarlet and organs, Kiyo Kaga oozed over the side, barely causing a ripple on his way to the bottom.

Pivoting, Davy sought the first warrior, the man whose hand he had broken. Rustling reeds marked where the warrior had just vanished. Davy eased onto his knees, glad the nightmare was finally over.

"Red Cheeks!" Wawaneechotinka said tenderly, throwing herself into his arms and bursting into tears.

Homecoming

For the longest while the only sounds were her heavy sobs. Davy let her cry herself dry, his arm over her shoulder. "I'm so sorry," he whispered several times. Once her warm lips brushed his and he responded, but only once.

They were huddled together when Flavius found them. Worried sick that his friend had been killed and he would have to find his way back to Tennessee by his lonesome, Flavius whooped for joy. "We did it!" he exclaimed. "Now we can head for home! Right, Davy?"

Davy Crockett absently nodded. But as he gazed out over the lush wilderness being bathed in the glow of the rising sun, he recollected being told about a tribe that lived to the west, a tribe that had piqued his curiosity. The Nadowessioux, some called them.

Maybe their gallivant was not quite over yet.